Who Says A Full House

Can't Beat A Smith & Wesson?

And Five Short Stories

G. L. O'CONNOR

ISBN: 0983528500
ISBN 13: 9780983528500

Very special thanks to Lee.

Without his efforts

my book would never have

reached your hand.

———

Thanks, also, to the other members of our

North Country Word Wranglers Writers Club

for their consistent critiques and encouragement.

CHAPTER 1

Taking the short cut to Blainey this early in the spring, with Temporary Creek running full with spring melt, was probably one of the stupidest thing I've done in a long time. It ranked right up there with my having held the reins of Ted Cooley's and Pete Ward's horses outside of the Blainey bank six years ago. I should have known better.

They were always pullin' something on me. But I was seventeen and stupid. By the way, my name is Jack Brannick. On the rolls at Laramie prison I'm listed as "John Carmody Brannick, Bank Robber, Pardoned." That's mostly correct.

Ted and Pete hadn't bothered to mention to me that they were joining the Custis brothers who were already inside the bank. The four of them were plannin' to rob the place. Not the smartest thing they'd ever done, either I'll tell you though, I didn't hold those reins long.

Inside the bank Willie Belcher the teller, who was certain he was being groomed for better things to come and so had begun to feel that this was his bank, grabbed the short-barreled pistol kept in his cash drawer. With trembling hands he fired almost point blank at

Nig Custis, somehow missing him completely. Then Willie promptly fainted inside his teller's cage.

But the damage had been done. The shot had been heard by Bill and Lud King, two of the best lawmen in Wyoming Territory, who were standing just across the street in front of the town jail.

The bullet broke the front window of the bank on its way out, burned the neck of Pete's brown stallion and just barely missed my ear. The animal bolted and so did I. The horse ran for home and I ran for cover, leaving Ted's horse to do as it damn. . . uh .. darn well pleased.

Inside the bank Willie's pistol shot had startled the felonious foursome so badly that they just stood there looking at each other. They had expected no resistance, so they had no plan of action other than to take the money and run. Run? Even that was stupid 'cause everybody in town knew who they were.

What's more, none of this bumbling band was a real leader. Not even Nig who was the oldest, and considered the wisest. These boys were certainly not the "Hole In The Wall" gang. Their robbery scheme was doomed from the start.

The King brothers knew the brain power of the would-be bandits, and the bandits were well aware of the keen abilities of the two lawmen so they knew better than to resist. Bill and Lud walked into the bank with their pistols in hand and calmly disarmed the four.

Then, just as calmly, they escorted them across the dusty street to the jail where they would wait upon the pleasure of the "Honorable" Judge Odell Richardson, the local imprudent dispenser of jurisprudence. Me, I was still behind the water trough in front of the bank.

Quite often the quality of the jurisprudence dispensed by "His Honor" depended on any of several things such as whether or not he liked the accused, the length of the trial, his mood, the heat of the day, his degree of soberness or how long that sobriety had been forced to last.

Thinking of the judge even now, six undeserved prison years later, still makes my temperature rise a notch and my blood move a little faster. Much the same as his desirable and receptive daughter did for me that many years ago, but for entirely different reasons.

Eldora Richardson, or "adorable Dorrie" as we young hot bloods of Blainey called her, was the prettiest girl in Wyoming Territory, as far as I was concerned. She was soon to be seventeen and beginning to strain the buttons on her blouse. Every inch of me, from the holes in my dirty socks to my shaggy uncut hair, was hopelessly in love with her.

I had spent every Sunday afternoon of the past two months sitting in her parlor looking calf-eyed at her. Of course, with the judge sitting just across the room reading and scowling, I couldn't do much more than that.

As it turned out, I was the only boy in town who foolishly wasted his time in the Richardson's parlor. Several others came calling after dark and met Dorrie in the grove behind her house. In fact, she was often already there waiting for them. Receptively!

I had no idea of this, at the time. I was not only naive and blind, but stupid as well. I was the only caller the judge was aware of and the one he had least reason to be concerned about. But he wasn't any smarter than I was where "adorable Dorrie" was concerned. I was the target of all his venom.

Part of the reason for the judge's dislike for me was the fact that I was more than six feet tall, and the Judge was about five feet five when he stretched. He hated looking up to younger people. Add to that my lack of "proper substance." I had no "pedigree." No family of note.

My dad, also named Jack Brannick, was the younger of two brothers on a Minnesota farm only large enough for one. He and my mother were heading west to Dakota Territory with farming on their minds when they heard of the gold being panned in streams in Wyoming Territory, so they drove their four-horse team and wagon across Dakota to Cheyenne and Laramie.

I was told that my dad had been a good farmer, was a better-than-average shot with pistol and rifle, but no hand at all where finding gold was concerned.

After a while he arranged for my mother to stay with Elmer and Gerda Haaken – an older couple of friends – while he went on further west in search of the gold he had not found in the Medicine Bow area northwest of Laramie. He figured to be gone two months. Six at the most. Mom had not told Dad that she was already several months pregnant.

Some bad things happened to Mom when I was getting born. She died when I was just a few weeks old without having been able to write to tell Dad about me. Nobody could figure why Dad never came back but he had heard about Mom dying and, not knowin' I even existed, he decided not to return to Medicine Bow and just kept on riding west. I grew up without knowing either of them.

When I was about two the Haakens gave up trying to raise anything on their small farm full of rocks and went back to Indiana where they belonged. They left me with county officials who could find a place for me to live until Dad came back.

From then on I lived in a lot of different homes in a lot of different towns. Some good, some not so good. Most all of these towns had schools, and the county folks made sure I attended, like it or not. That's how come I can read and write. That's how I came to be living in Blainey.

Every time one of the families I'd be living with would pull stakes or prove unfit the King brothers, acting for the county, would take me into their home until they could find another place for me.

Sometimes I'd be with them for a few days, other times a few weeks. I told them I'd like to live with them permanently. I believe I was twelve that year. They liked the idea, too, but their lawman duties kept them running so much to all parts of the territory that they felt they couldn't give me a good home.

Off and on, over the next several years I was with them quite a bit. I learned a lot about what not to do with guns and knives, when to duck and when to stand ground, and how to tell by the look in a man's eyes or how he carried himself whether he was dangerous or scared. They were my favorite teachers, bar none.

I said they taught me what not to do with knives and guns. Of course, in order to teach me that they also had to teach me a lot about what I should do with them. This was the part I liked best.

They taught me how to shoot with pistol and rifle, and they did a good job. I got so that I could turn quick and shoot straight. Jonas said I'd have made a fearsome outlaw.

The King brothers were born Jonas, Wilhelm and Ludvig Koehnig in Bitterburg, Germany, a small town north of Hannover, where their father Rheinholt was a clock maker and goldsmith well-known for his ability and honesty.

The family emigrated to America arriving in Boston in 1860 where Rhino Koehnig had expected to gain employment in the Waltham watch and clock factory.

The first shots of the Civil War had just been fired at Fort Sumter so Rhino moved his young family further west as fast as he could, settling first in Ohio and finally in Sterling, Colorado. He Americanized his name by changing it to King, which is what Koehnig means in German.

Rhino and Frieda King raised their sons in the strong, strict German traditions of hard work and honesty. It was my good fortune to have received much benefit of their old world training. Again, like it or not.

The brothers moved to Wyoming Territory where they became lawmen. Jonas was twenty-four, Will was twenty-three and Lud was twenty-two.

About this same time straight-backed, no-nonsense Miss Mary Lynn Berg of Madison, Wisconsin, in her high-bodiced dresses with white collars and her tightly wound and bound blonde hair, came west to teach the young people of Wyoming Territory how to read and write. And maybe find a husband while she was about it.

One day, after reading one of my theme papers, she surprised me with a fine compliment. "John Brannick," her back as straight as a rod, her hair in a bun so tight on the back of her head her face hadn't skin left for smiling, "You don't know a gerund from a participle and are not, it seems, disposed to learn the difference, but you certainly do know how to use them."

She came close to smiling just then and I thought maybe she's not really all that bad. It was things like that kept me in school a lot longer than I was "disposed" to be there.

Pocket money for a kid in my situation was pretty scarce so I did a lot of odd jobs for folks around Blainey. I carried a lot of groceries and things for widows and oldsters, helped unload the dray wagons and split firewood for folks. I got a nickel or dime here and there. Lots of the older ladies paid me in cookies.

I often helped Mick Shane unload beer and whiskey kegs in back of his saloon and roll them down into the cellar underneath. It was damp and cool down there and smelled great.

I once asked Mick, "Don'tcha ever lock the door back here?"

He grinned. "Sometimes. The regular door I keep barred," he said. "But this cellar door – most folks know it's kinda dangerous comin' in here in the dark so I don't have to worry."

He was right about that. There were just two rails to roll the barrels down. Off to one side there was a steep set of very narrow steps. Otherwise, the place was just a dark hole about six feet deep. If you didn't know where to find those steps you could break your neck.

Mick had a table upstairs he'd lay out with bread, cheese and spiced meats each noon and suppertime so his drinkers and gamblers could catch a cheap meal without having to interrupt their pursuit of the activities that kept Mick in business. After helping him unload the barrels and kegs we would often sit in the cool basement and eat one of his huge sandwiches.

Once I helped Mick lift a whiskey keg up through the trapdoor in the floor behind the bar. Most people didn't know about the trapdoor.

He told me, "Sometimes a cowboy gets liquored up an' starts shootin' the place full o' holes. I just open the trap and jump down here nice an' safe."

For helpin' him one day he gave me a quarter and my first taste of beer. The stuff smelled a whole lot better than it tasted, I can tell you.

When Bill King came to the Richardson's front door that Sunday afternoon wearin' his badge, the judge knew it was a business call. They stepped out onto the porch leaving Dorrie an' me alone.

Dorrie slid over from her end of the sofa and rounded her shoulders forward so that I could see down into her blouse, if I cared to. Of course I cared to. I'm sure my eyes must have bulged nearly out of my head.

I decided to try kissing her, which I had never done before. She smiled when I came close to her, face to face. She grabbed my head with both her hands and pressed her mouth on mine real hard. Our teeth hit together so hard I thought they'd break.

I heard the creak of the screen door as the judge started back inside. I turned to look just as Dorrie tried to bite my lip. She bit my cheek instead. That made her all mad an' stormy an' she pushed away.

I don't know why some people do the things they do. 'Specially girls. Don't know why she wanted to bite my lip but she was grinnin' with a wild look in her eyes when she tried. It was when she realized she got me on the face, instead, that she got mad. Hurt like hell, too.

The judge noticed that Dorrie had not quite made it all the way back to her end of the couch and he scowled at me. You could tell he figured that whatever had been going on must surely have been my doing. It never occurred to him that his dear darling Dorrie was anything less than angelic.

"Time you were leaving, Muddy," he scowled. My middle name is Carmody, and if you say it fast enough it sounds like CAR-muddy. As many folks around called me Muddy as called me Jack. The judge thought I didn't like the name so he used it on me all the time. Actually, there were several men in the area with the name of Jack, but I was the only Muddy. I liked it.

Before I dared stand up I grabbed my old hat. With my thumb hooked over my belt buckle I kept the hat squarely in front of me to cover the bulge in my britches as I sidled toward the door.

I don't think I fooled the judge one little bit, though, 'cause after that every time he saw me his expression turned from whatever it had been to a real storm cloud of a scowl.

It was at about this time – the time of the bank robbery trial – that the judge learned of Dorrie's nighttime rendezvous in the grove, from which she often returned with tousled hair and messed up clothing.

Since I was the only one of her callers he knew about, the judge assumed that I was the nighttime bandit. His dislike for me became hatred. I was told, in no uncertain terms, not to call again at the Richardson home.

It was also about that same time I learned about Dorie's evening activities in the grove, too. For maybe half an hour I was heartbroken, then I was mad as hell that I had "missed out."

Terp Finley, one of the guys my age, noticed my swollen cheek and made comment. "See Dorrie gotcha." He said it with a chuckle and a knowing look. "That girl is goofy, always bitin' like that. Don't know why I keep botherin' with her."

"Well, if she's gonna do that to you, why do you go there?" I asked him.

"Well now, jist why do y' think?" When he saw by the stupid look on my face that I really didn't understand, he snorted, "Jeez, Muddy. Don't you know nuthin'?" I had never liked Terp and when he made me feel foolish or stupid, like right now, I liked him even less.

CHAPTER 2

My friends' trial was held in Wheatland which was about fifty or sixty miles north of Cheyenne, the territorial capitol. Blainey was about midway between Wheatland and Fort Laramie, a distance of maybe fifteen miles.

Judge Richardson had his choice of two places in town to convene his court. Either the school house or the Ten Strike saloon. The saloon smelled of stale beer, spittoon juice, dead cigar butts and ashes but it was larger, cooler and closer to the jail. Everyone knew the judge was a "thirsty man" so no one was surprised when he chose the saloon.

In the course of the trial Ted Cooley passed the remark, "Me an' Pete talked Muddy into holdin' our horses for us whilst we went into the bank to help make the 'withdrawal.' " He laughed. So did everyone else. Except Judge Richardson.

He pounced on that bit of testimony as his weapon of vengeance. The means by which he could rid himself of the one he thought was his daughter's secret lover.

"Deputies," he roared at the King brothers as he pointed at me. "I order you to arrest this young hellion as an accessory to the crime of bank robbery." I was sitting right there in the barroom, a stupid kid of seventeen. I didn't know what was going on.

Bill and Lud figured the judge had gone crazy. First they tried to calm him down and get him to reconsider. When they realized how serious he was they finally did as they had been ordered to do, but that afternoon they telegraphed Jonas to come up from Cheyenne to help with my defense. He was on hand when court re-convened the next morning

Jonas had been studying law while serving as sheriff of Laramie county, although I don't know when he found time for it. At that time Laramie County covered nearly a third of Wyoming Territory. Jonas often spent day and night in the saddle spreading law and order across the land. And whatever territory Jonas couldn't cover by himself his brothers did.

No matter what or where the crime, one of the King brothers was usually there to settle the situation, or bring the guilty in for trial. Bill and Lud were Jonas's chief deputies.

Although Ted, Pete and both of the Custis brothers swore that I'd had nothing to do with the robbery, Judge Richardson dismissed their testimony as the word of "known robbers," and my "cohorts" in the crime, and therefore unreliable and inadmissible.

The King brothers assured the judge that I'd had no part in the incident, but he refused to listen. Jonas made several legal sounding protests but his small grasp of formal law was no match for the judge's knowledge and experience, nor for his deviousness and wrath. All five of us were quickly found guilty.

"Peter Ward and Theodore Cooley," Judge Richardson boomed in his 'I-am-God-Almighty' voice, "you are herewith sentenced to twenty years in the territorial penitentiary at Laramie." Ted's mouth sagged open and Pete plopped down into his chair, staring.

"Nigel and Brutus Custis," the judge continued, "You are likewise sentenced to serve twenty years in the territorial penitentiary." Bru started to cry. Nig just stared at the floor, like Pete.

Then the judge looked at me. The satisfaction that showed in his eyes was frightening. My heart froze. Even before he said the words I knew I was going to prison, too. "And finally you, John Carmody Brannick," his red face glowing with his victory as he expounded with dramatic eloquence.

"For your complicity in aiding and abetting these four criminals in their felonious attack upon the financial security of the unsuspecting citizens of the Blainey community, I sentence you to serve twenty years in the territorial prison at Laramie." The judge loved to spew out large, legal sounding words.

Jonas was on his feet in an instant. "No!" he shouted. "No!" He rushed to the judge's bench, which in this case was a green, felt-covered faro table. Lowering his voice enough that others wouldn't hear, he told Judge Richardson through gritted teeth, "Change that sentence on the Brannick boy. Do it now. Do it! Or I'll expose you right here and now."

"Blackmail?" the judge leered, also keeping his voice low. "The pure and saintly Sheriff King is going to stoop to blackmail? And in the name of the law? Now won't that look good in the newspaper."

The judge had the unpleasant habit of leering when he knew he had the upper hand. Or thought he had. But Jonas wasn't quite through yet.

He leaned close to the judge's purple-veined face and softly whispered, "Mavis Wertin." At the sound of that name I saw the judge's head jerk and his face lose some of its purple color. "Change the sentence," Jonas whispered again. "Now!"

I know Jonas had not intended for me to overhear, but I was the closest to the faro table 'cause I was the last one sentenced. I'm sure the others didn't catch the name.

The judge stared at Jonas for a few seconds while color, perspiration and anger returned to his whiskey-bloated face. He picked up his gavel and grimly rapped on the green tabletop, calling for order. He addressed the gathering as if he were continuing with his previous remarks.

"However," he wheezed, "in view of Mister Brannick's youth and the fact that this is his first appearance before this court, the court sees fit to proceed leniently." Jonas began to relax. "I hereby suspend half of his sentence reducing it to ten years at Laramie Prison."

Jonas started forward again but His Honor brought the gavel down hard and fast on the faro table. "Court's adjourned," he barked. "Bar's open."

The trial was over and we were going to prison! And for what? I hadn't done anything. I had always disliked the judge, but now I hated him. And I was scared. Someone in the room laughed. It was Dorrie!

CHAPTER 3

Brick-walled Laramie Territorial Prison first opened its doors in 1872. When we arrived in the spring of '79 the place had been up and running for almost seven years. The warden was Gustav Schnitger, a fair-but-firm bristle-faced former Prussian whose rigid posture suggested a military background.

There were eight of us in the caged wagon that brought us to Laramie Prison: the five of us from Blainey, and three tough looking men from the Cheyenne area who already seemed to know each other.

The warden met us at the prison door. He wasn't smiling or frowning as he stood with feet apart, his hands in back of his swallow-tailed coat with two armed guards on each side of him.

"Chentlemen," he said with audible accent. He always used that term when he addressed his prisoners. "Follow me." He confidently turned his back on us and led the way into the receiving room, or "guest room" as it was often called.

Behind us the large, heavy outer doors of the prison thudded shut. Now we were really in prison. I felt a little sick. I wanted to cry but I didn't dare.

First the warden addressed the three men from Cheyenne in a flat tone of voice. "Krain, Steele and Dunn, I had hoped I'd never see you three again. That maybe you'd change your ways. Or get yourselves killed in some alley in Cheyenne." He didn't smile, but exhaled in disgust and disappointment.

"Vell, your stay viss us this time vill not be as pleasant as the last." He turned to two of the guards. "Escort these three chentlemen to the north wing. If they make any sudden moves on you . . . shoot them." It was easy to see that the three men believed him. I surely did.

"Don't remove their irons until they've been stripped and searched and are secure inside their cells." With their chains dragging and rattling across the brick floor the three hard-looking men scuffed out of the room doing the 'Laramie Half-step,' also called the 'Chain Gang Shuffle.'

Then the warden lined us up and took the time to look each of us over. One of the guards stood next to him holding a cocked pistol aimed loosely in our direction. The other guard stood across the room, his short-barrelled shotgun held in the same casual manner.

I was the last in line and probably looked a whole lot younger and scareder than the others. I was only four years younger than Bru Custis but I'm sure I was a lot scareder. When the warden looked at me he took a step back, looked at the others again, then back at me. I was taller than any of them but didn't hardly weigh a hundred and forty pounds.

"Vhat are you doing here, young man?" he asked. We all noticed that he had called me 'young man' instead of using my last name, or even the number I had just been assigned as he had with the others.

Before I could answer Nig spoke up. Being the oldest Nig had sort of taken over as head shepherd of our little flock. "Sir. Uh . . . Warden. Muddy, he don't really belong here at all. And Judge Richardson knows it, too," Nig said, defending me. "But the judge purely hates Muddy 'cause he thinks he's been messin' with his daughter."

Warden Schnitger hardly moved his head when he looked at Nig. His voice was quiet but hard. "Who gave you permission to speak?" Nig blinked in surprise, started to answer, then decided against it.

The warden, without any change of expression and still looking at Nig, muttered "Thank you. I haff met the judge." There was disgust in his voice. "And now, chentlemen, let us discuss your stay with us."

He told us of our duties, warned us of punishments for infractions, assigned us cells and cell mates and gave us basic instructions on work details and other such things. He preferred conducting these first meetings with new "guests" himself, rather than having it done by his staff.

Then he ordered us to strip, and witnessed our being searched. The search was carried out by others of his personnel while the guards watched. With no clothes on I was too embarrassed to look at the others.

While we were getting into our prison uniforms, Warden Schnitger addressed us again in his chillingly soft voice. "Chentlemen, it is my hope that it will never be necessary for me to see you face to face again . . . unless I send for you."

He turned and stiffly walked from the room, his short, tapered beard pointing the way. I think everyone of us was certain that this quiet man would order us shot in a second for whatever reason.

———◆———

They put all five of us in the same section, called cell block B, but in separate cells with assigned cellmates. I was taken to my cell by a thick-chested man named Krieger. I learned later that the prisoners called him "The German" because he kept his hair cut short like a Hussar.

I also learned that he was cruel and that he enjoyed using his club, a piece of oak about two feet long, which he 'applied' across a man's back or to the side of his head. He also seemed to "like" younger men . . . like me.

Just before we reached my cell the German halted, faced me, ran his hand slowly down my arm and said, "I can make things tough or easy for you. You be nice to me an' I'll take care of you. Otherwise," he slapped his open palm with his club. "Understand?" I didn't know what he meant so I just looked at him. Then he stepped aside. "O.K. Into your cage."

I shared my cell with the biggest and blackest man I'd ever seen. Actually, I had never seen a black man before. I had no idea what to expect of him. As I said, I'm a bit over six feet tall but this man towered over me. I was mighty scared and careful when I introduced myself.

"Uh . . . hello," I stammered, extending my hand. "I'm John Brannick. Some people call me Jack and others call me by my nickname of Muddy. But you can call me whatever you like." As if I could stop you, I thought.

"Evenin' Mistah Muddy," this huge man said with a smile and a manner that eased my mind a lot. Even though he tried to speak softly his big voice boomed like the bottom keys on a church organ. "I be Bojo," he said.

When we shook hands his callouses felt like the scales on a fish's belly. This man had done his share of hard work "My right an' proper name be Joseph Beaujoulais. Dat be too much f' mos' folks roun' here so dey jis' call me Joe or Bojo. Some say Nigger Joe. I don't much like dat one, though. Don' like the way they says it."

I don't know if the relief I was feeling just then was showing in my face but I certainly felt it inside of me. Joe was a giant, but a gentle one. I was able to smile genuinely when I said, "I'm pleased to meet you, Mr. Beaujoulais. Uh...Joseph."

He smiled.. "Be pleased you call me Joe or Bojo," he informed me. His smile lit up the cell. "You be jes' in time for supper." It would be difficult not to like this man. After that I called him Joe sometimes, Bojo other times.

"Oh, supper? What do I do?" I hadn't eaten in several hours and was really hungry.

"You jis' keep close an' do what I do." he advised. "You be awright." Then he asked a strange question. "Can you read, John?"

I said, "How'd be if you called me Muddy, Joe? Yes, I can read."

"I can't. Don' know my numbers too good, neither. Don' know how ol' I be. I don't be old yet, but I don' be young no mo, too. But mos'ly I'd like to read. Man, dat be gooood." He said the last word slowly.

The prison dining area was at the north end of this north-to-south building. We could see it through the bars of our cell. The main door of the prison, the one through which we had entered when we arrived that first day, was out of sight behind us.

The north wing, where the three Cheyenne men had been taken, extended west from the mess hall. I wondered why they didn't call it the west wing.

Someone blew a whistle and the cell doors were cranked open by some kind of pulley system. Joe had to dip his head to go through the door, then he stepped out and to one side. I did the same and stepped to the other side of our cage door.

The whistle blew again and I followed him to my first prison meal. This became one of several routines. The guard's whistles controlled our lives.

Each morning we were awakened by reveille, which was the sound of every guard in the cell block blowing his whistle. If you were on a work detail you started work when you heard a whistle. Or another whistle made you stop what you were doing and got you ready to do something else. The whistles woke you, fed you, started you, stopped you and put you to bed.

CHAPTER 4

For the next several days I copied everything Joe did, except when we were on work detail. Nobody could match him when it came to work. Most of us were given five-pound sledge hammers with which to break rocks. Joe effortlessly swung a nine-pounder against rock all day long, three days a week, singing sea chanties and African chants.

Another three days each week he worked in the kitchen, his favorite place. He liked to cook Because he was a model prisoner he was given one day a week to loaf. Very few others had earned this reward.

The five of us, being new prisoners, were assigned to the rock pile everyday. Our hands bled, blistered and healed over many times until they looked like Joe's scaly palms. I was luckier than the others. I had Joe to help me.

He always managed to have a stash of lard from the kitchen or wheel grease from the delivery wagons. With his huge hands he massaged these ointments into my bleeding palms each night. I often fell asleep while he was doing this. By morning I was always able to handle my five-pounder, break more rock and build more blisters.

After several weeks of this duty we began to work "two-dayers," or "two-ees." We would alternate two days on the rock pile and two days in the broom or furniture factory. Both of the factories were housed in separate buildings inside the prison walls.

The constant routine began to blur the weeks and months so that I never sure what day it was. There were no Sundays here.

When we'd been in prison a couple of weeks The German came to our cell after lock-up and lights-out, and took me out. Bojo was scared for me. He said, "Don't be hurtin' this boy, German."

Krieger snarled back, "Mind your own damn business, Nigger."

He took me to the room where they often questioned prisoners. He made it clear to me that I was to be his "playmate" and that I could cooperate or suffer the consequences. I didn't cooperate. He didn't use his club on me, but he didn't need to. I was a prisoner and he was a guard. I knew better than to fight back.

Using his fists he hit me everywhere but on my face, where it might show. He told me this would keep on happening until I got my thinking "straightened out." Then he took me back to my cell.

Bojo helped me into my bunk, where I spent a painful night, and he helped me out of it in the morning. The first two or so hours of rock pounding that day were painful and slow. Of course, Bojo passed along to the others word of what had happened to me.

———◆———

Strenuous and painful though the work was, the worst part of being in prison was the nighttime in the near-black darkness of the cell. I knew I wasn't supposed to be there and that made my nights even longer and heavier. I often cried myself to sleep It helped when Joe and I talked until one of us fell asleep.

One night I asked him, "Joe, I've never heard anybody talk just like you. What part of the country are you from?"

"I be fum Af'ica, Muddy," he answered.

"Afika?" I stupidly replied. "Oh, Africa! Africa! My gosh, Joe! How'd yuh get here?" Joe took so long to answer that I thought he had gone to sleep. Then his big voice softly rumbled in the darkness,

"Some mans come to our village. Kill old people, take young mans an' womans. Take us on ship-boats over long water," There was a change in his voice. I realized it pained him to recall. "Dey take Bee-Rah away. Dey take my woman away."

I thought his woman's name was Vera, then he said it again. "Dey take Bee-Rah. She be sold somewheres. I be sold 'nudder somewheres." He was quiet again.

Here I was feeling sorry for myself over being sent to prison. It's true that was bad, but I'd get out after a while. Joe had lost everything. His family and his whole way of life. And Bee-Rah. After a long moment I asked, "They took her away?"

"Not so far," he said. "One day I see Bee-Rah workin' in d' nex' field. I run to her. Da 'seer-boss' he try to stop me. He ride his horse at me an' swing da whip at me an' at Bee-Rah." In the darkness I could feel him moving on his bunk. It excited him to talk about it.

Joe yanked the overseer from his horse and hit him hard. Then he mounted the horse, lifted Bee-rah up behind him and galloped out of the field. The other field workers were afraid to cheer but they smiled. Several waved their hoes in the air. None of them offered to help the overseer who had not yet been able to get to his feet.

With the help of other slaves who hid and fed them, they traveled up from Texas, across Oklahoma Kansas and Colorado, finally reaching Cheyenne before they felt safe enough to try to ask for work.

Joe didn't know that he had crossed several states. He only knew where the seer-boss was and he went away from him.

Again Joe paused so long in his story that I thought he had gone to sleep. I began to nod off when his big voice startled me awake. "Muddy, do it be hard to learn to read?"

CHAPTER 5

In late September my spirits got a great boost. It was a letter from Jonas King: It had already been opened, of course. By prison people, I supposed.

Dear Jack.

> I am working on getting your sentence revoked. I don't know enough about the law to be much good yet, but I am learning. I will keep at it. Don't give up hope.
>
> Your warden is a friend of mine. We met through our duties with the law. He is a fair man. Keep your nose clean and you'll be all right. If you need anything let me know. Regards.

Jns King

I wrote back asking him to send me some paper, pen and ink so that I could try my hand at teaching Bojo to read. Also I thought I'd keep a journal.

Evidently out-going letters were read, too, 'cause it was right about then that I was called into the warden's office and given a paper full of questions to answer. I think it was just to see if I could read and write well enough to be of use to the warden.

My two-ees of broom making changed to two days of clerking, sometimes in the factories, sometimes in the warden's office. Of course I still had to pull my regular two-ee on the rock pile. Warden Schnitger didn't let his prisoners get soft.

A person's mind can get pretty soft, too, if he doesn't make use of it. One of the things we did to keep sharp was to make rhymes of as many things as we could. Working on the rock pile became "rock knocking." My office duties were called "clerk work."

Everyone was trying to name things. In cell block A they called the infirmary "ill hill," and getting yourself sent there was called "pulling a sick trick." Anything to keep from going crazy. I had a big advantage. I had a student to teach.

At first I felt pretty foolish leading this huge man through the alphabet making the same sounds that I remembered my teachers making for us when we were kids of six and seven. I soon realized, however, that nothing I did was too basic for Bojo. Although he could speak the language, he had no idea what his words looked like.

At one point I wondered if Joe might be a simpleton, a name I'd heard someone call a boy who had fallen from a loft as a child, striking his head. Not Joe. He could cajole and manipulate everyone around him. Even the warden. He was certainly not simple. And he was liked by everyone. All except one: the man called Krain who had arrived in the prison ambulance with us.

I heard Krain speak to Bojo during one of our short work breaks. Krain walked up to him and said, "Well, lookee who we got here. It's that big nigger I said I was gonna kill." He looked at Joe with a crazy kind of grin. His eyes scared me.

"And I'm gonna getcha this time, Nigger," he lowered his voice. "Ol' Warden Gus turned me loose last time before I could get to you. Not this time." Then he walked away. Joe's expression never changed. I was sure that he could have squashed Krain like a bug, but he didn't move.

I aked Bojo why Krain wanted to kill him. He answered, "Do' know. I think it be 'cause I be black an' he be white." Bojo was the first black man I had ever met. I didn't understand hating someone as gentle as he.

Along with the paper, pen and ink I'd asked him for, Jonas King had sent me three "penny dreadfuls," those popular ten-cent short novels, printed on rough paper, about heroes, villains, cowboys and Indians of the western plains.

People in the eastern part of the country couldn't get their fill of stories of our wild and wooly west. It was amazing what they would believe, fact or fiction. And nobody seemed to know why something that cost a dime could be called penny dreadfuls.

Everyone in the cellblock enjoyed hearing me read them aloud through the bars at night. Especially Joe. Afterward, holding one of the booklets in his hand Joe would point to a word and ask me, "What be dis word, Muddy?"

Then he would look at it and say the word over several times. Almost every night, before the last whistle, we spent a few minutes sounding out and looking at words.

One February day, when it was too cold for rock knocking, we were making "cheap sweeps," in the broom factory. Bojo was looking at a three-word sign. There was the strain of concentration in his face as he sounded out the words. "Doe....note....spite."

He labored through it again. Then he let out a terrible yell. "I GOT IT! I KNOW WHAT DAT SAY! 'DO - NOT - SPIT'." He laughed and shouted it all again.

Everyone in the prison knew that big Bojo was trying to read. Most of the men in the factory that day knew what had just happened and many of them laughed along with Joe. Some of them even applauded. Joe read the sign aloud again. His smile was huge.

———◆———

I saw Ted, Pete and the Custis boys every day during "dime time" – the ten-minute breaks we got while knocking rocks. The longer we were in prison the more we felt cut off from our own world so we had become closer friends inside the high walls.

Nig Custis had assumed the role of protective leader of our small group. He was the biggest and oldest of the five of us and not afraid of anything.

Having Bojo around I didn't really need any extra protection, but Nig had already gotten into a couple of scrapes sticking up for each of us. He confronted "The wormin' German" and told him to leave Bru and me alone. Krieger didn't try to use his club on Nig. I think he was afraid of him. Word of that got around, too.

One day Nig was getting a bale of twine from the broom factory tack room. When he turned he saw that he was cornered by three men. One of them was Krain. The other two were his Cheyenne friends who had arrived at the prison with us. They grabbed Nig and held him while Krain beat him badly with his work-toughened fists.

Krain snarled at Nig, "I'm the tough guy around here. You remember that." Nig sagged to the floor as Krain and his men walked away.

Nig should have been sent to the infirmary for his injuries, but when he wouldn't tell the warden who'd beaten him – jailbirds don't sing – the warden let him lick his own wounds and made him take his regular two-ees, rock pile and all.

A month later – it was full spring in 1880 and I was now eighteen – Lud and Bill King came to Laramie to deliver a prisoner. They asked to see all five of us. Usually visitors only get to see one convict at a time, but because Lud and Bill were lawmen and known to the warden, he took all five of us off our work details and let us visit with them.

The first thing the King boys noticed was how scarred Nig's face was. Nig wouldn't tell them about it, but we did.

"Krain? That lunatic?" Bill King was surprised. "He's in here? You boys be careful around him. He's nuts."

Lud asked Nig, "You're not plannin' on gettin' even with him, are you?" When Nig said he damn sure was Lud advised, "Better forget it. Please!" he stressed. "The man is crazy. Even if you win you'll eventually lose because he'll never forget. He won't just get even. He'll kill you. Really. Just forget about it."

Then we settled down to visiting and asking about people we knew and such things. They told us that Jonas was still working on getting my sentence overturned, and that he was working on getting the others' sentences reduced. We all felt better after their visit.

CHAPTER 6

About this time I decided to try writing my own dreadful. Everybody was tired of listening to the same ones being read aloud and being passed around so I thought I'd try my hand at writing a new one.

At first I didn't tell anyone because I wasn't sure I could do it. By the time I was satisfied with it, it was mid-summer. It was fifty-one pages long and I read it aloud one night to all the guys in our cell block. I called the story "One-Eyed Jacks."

It was about a poker game in a mining camp. A young miner and several others were losing their dust to two card sharks who used marked cards and secret signals. But the cheaters got their signals mixed and each one began to think the other was trying to cheat him.

There was a gunfight in which the cheaters shot each other. The only one still in the game when the smoke cleared was the young miner who was declared winner of whatever was on the table.

It was a good story. There were winners and losers. There was a gunfight. The bad guys lost and the good guy won. The whole cell block liked it. Some even clapped. They all wanted to hear it again. I felt great.

In the next week I read it aloud to them three more times and I immediately began writing another. By the middle of winter I had completed four more.

Middle of winter? Already?

Every so often it would happen like that. I'd do or say something that would remind me where we were and how our lives had changed. We'd been at Laramie a year and a half by this time. Had we changed?

Well, not Ted and Pete. They seemed to ride the current whichever way it carried them, much the same as they had back in Blainey.

Nig and Bru had both changed, though. Ever since the beating from Krain and his helpers Nig had become quieter and moodier. We all worried that he was watching for his opportunity to take his revenge.

Bru saw this, too, and became more watchful and protective of his big brother, trying always to be working close by him. Bru was growing up. And he was getting tougher both in body and mind. Being in prison definitely toughens your mind.

I hadn't grown any taller than I was the day we got to Laramie; still a couple inches over six feet. But all that rock knocking I'd been doing and the meat and beans the warden was feeding us had really beefed me up.

I was somethin' over a hundred and ninety pounds and my hands were just like Bojo's, now. So tough you could hardly pound a nail through them. The rest of me had gotten pretty tough, too.

We learned to take your lickings without crying to the warden. Or to anyone else, for that matter. So when The German finally did use his club on Nig we didn't snitch and Nig didn't complain.

It happened when we were all rock knocking. The wormin' German caught up to me when I was at the water barrel. "I'll be by tonight for your next lesson, Brannick." Nig overheard him and gave him a strong unfriendly warning. "You leave Muddy and Bru alone or I'll break you in half."

The German's face showed fear and then anger. He was afraid of Nig but angry that a prisoner dared to talk to him like that. Nig turned to walk away. Krieger, using both hands, brought his club across Nig's back. The blow was so forceful it sent Nig to the ground. Krieger raised the club to hit again.

"No!" It was Locks, the head guard. "The man's down. No need to kill him. Not on my watch, anyway. What did he do?"

"None o' yer damn business," Krieger snarled and stomped away. We formed a ring around Nig and helped him to his feet. Injured or not, he still had to work.

———————◆———————

A prison is not a community. It is a group of individuals. Individual murderers, thieves, rapists, embezzlers, robbers . . . and several innocents, like me. It's a terrible place.

Every day you are standing next to or bumping up against a man who had raped or robbed someone. Or brutally assulted someone. They are not nice people.

Here again I was the lucky one. I had Bojo to protect me. Even so, I saw, heard and was in the midst of trouble every day. It changes you. After a while you stop being scared. You become alert; learn to read signs; you're always ready to handle whatever or whoever comes your way.

The "northend" prisoners, the really dangerous ones, were usually kept separated from the rest of us, but sometimes during rest periods or on trips to the water barrel a man can wander.

Krain, with his two goons for protection, came looking for someone to beat up so that he could improve his reputation as top tough guy.

We were ready for him this time. We weren't the same timid flock of sheep we were the day we had arrived.

Krain spotted Nig and decided to give him a repeat lesson, but Bru and I were there. Bru blocked the path of one of the goons and I stepped in front of the other. Nig wasted no time in taking care of Krain who, like most bullies, was a coward when alone.

Nig's first punch was a beauty, a fist hard into Krain's belly. His breath whooshed out so loud I thought he was going to throw up.

Then Nig hit him with a left to the right side of his face that snapped his head to the side and caused his knees to buckle slightly.

Then a right fist, and another, and a third into his face destroying parts of it.

Finally, Nig moved his left foot a half step back to brace himself, and fired his left fist deep into Krain's stomach, this time forcing all his breath and some of his breakfast out through his nose and mouth.

His eyes, which Nig's fists had not touched, blazed insanely, then faded into glassy semi-consciousness. The two goons had been afraid to move with Bru and me standing ready to treat them in similar fashion.

When Nig stepped away from Krain, who was now lying on the ground in his own vomit and blood, it was Bru who spoke in a soft, dangerous tone I'd never heard him use before. "Now you can have him. Keep him out of our territory."

Krain's face and lips were so smashed that he couldn't speak much more than to gurgle "Kill you! Kill you!" Supported by the goons, he was stagger-carried away.

The entire action had taken only seconds, but even so we were all surprised that the guards didn't see or interfere. Oddly, they had all been looking away, and only after the action was over did they come toward us from several directions telling us that our break time was over and to get back to work.

The guard nearest Nig was smiling just a little – I knew that the guards hated Krain, too. Without looking at Nig he muttered, "Nice work. But you'll have to be real careful from now on."

We swung our sledges with pleasure the rest of that day, I'll tell you. And we had great tale-telling to do that night in the cell block.

I had felt no fear when I stepped in front of Krain's goon. I was ready to handle whatever followed. I wasn't a kid, anymore. I thought about that. It felt good.

That night after most of the others in block B had fallen asleep Joe quietly said to me, "You wins today, Muddy. But now you gots to look careful. Krain gonna kill you."

He was quiet for a moment then added, "His head don't be right, dat Krain. He crazy. You gots to look careful now." I wasn't cold and I don't think I was scared, but just the same I shivered.

CHAPTER 7

Thinking of my own story and feeling sorry for myself was what had gotten me interested in the stories of others in my block. They'd all heard me read my made-up dreadfuls, so I asked one of my block mates, a cattle thief named Tom Thick, if I could try making a tale using his story.

I said I would change it a bit here and there, maybe use a different name and possibly add a few things. He grinned and proudly made me promise to use his real name. That was the beginning.

I wrote "Tom Thick, Cattle Rustler." In my story vigilantes caught Tom with a herd of stolen cattle. He escaped and hid in a whore house. After a long chase and a shoot-out in a saloon, in which no one was killed although three vigilantes were wounded, they captured Thick and decided to string him up. That's when lawman Jonas King arrived in time to rescue him and take him away to Cheyenne for trial.

I gave it to Thick to read privately before reading it to the whole cell block. We were both red-faced when he had to tell me that he couldn't read. He wanted the tale to be read to the others so badly that he urged me to do it that night anyway.

The men laughed and hooted at different spots in the story, and Thick was as proud as a banty rooster. He yelled through the bars, "How'd yuh like the part about me hidin' in a whore house?" They all laughed and whooped again.

It soon became difficult to tell who was the more famous around the prison, the rustler or the author. After that everyone in our cell block wanted to tell me their story, urging me to use their real names in my dreadfuls.

Using real names and stories made it easier. I only had to make up half of the material. Sometimes less. Some months I wrote more than one a week. Some times only one or two in a month. By the time Jonas got me "graduated" four years later I had written sixty-two of them. And several of my "roommates" were famous.

Taylor Rosser, another of my cellblock "neighbors," was serving a two-to-ten sentence for involuntary manslaughter. In a poker game with a stranger and four friends he was holding a full house. It turned out that every man at that table was holding a 'winning hand.'

The stranger, a card shark, had dealt them to them. All were betting and raising in a fit of "gambler's fever". The stranger, of course, held the best hand. And a small Model One Smith and Wesson revolver.

The card shark's parting words, as he picked up their money, was, "Gentlemen, always remember, no poker hand beats a Smith and Wesson." But as he turned to leave, with their winnings in his pocket, Tay broke a chair over his head, accidentally killing him.

The title of his dreadful was, "A Smith and Wesson Beats A Full House, Every Time." The boys in the block loved it. So did Tay. I got it finished just before his parole came through.

———◆———

I was also gaining some stature as a teacher. My pupil Bojo, that huge, powerful, gentle giant, was learning to read. As he understood each of the placards posted throughout the prison – signs he had seen everyday but had not known how to decipher – he began to read them aloud. Then he'd laugh and repeat them. Joseph Beaujoulaise was a happy man. Tom Thick asked if I'd try teaching him, also.

Jonas had been selling my stories to a reporter he knew on a Baltimore newspaper. They had permission to sell them to other newspapers in return for royalties. My first story sold for fifty dollars. The sixty-second story brought four hundred dollars from the Baltimore paper plus another fifty from each newspaper they sold it to.

Jonas informed me that the account he had opened for me in the Cheyenne State Bank was getting pretty fat, and some of my cell block friends were becoming pretty famous. Or infamous.

The men were uproariously pleased when I told them all this through the cell bars. One of them yelled out, "Hey, rich man. How about a loan." The men all laughed.

Another hollered, "Yeah, me too. I want to hire a good lawyer t' get me the hell outta here." That got a really big laugh.

By now Jonas King had become an attorney and had gotten out of the sheriffing business, leaving that to brothers Bill and Lud. All three of them were the heroes of several of my yarns.

I didn't think to ask permission to use their names until my fourth "King" tale. By then they were enjoying their fame too, although they were a little embarrassed by it.

———◆———

"Muddy, y' gotcher-r-r-r self a visitor-r-r," Locks yelled across the rock yard in his Scottish brogue. My sledge and I were having a "discussion" with a big rock when he hollered.

"Warden says yar-r-r t' get on up t' the 'guest r-r-room' r-r-right away." We all liked to hear his musical, rattling speech.

"Thanks, Locks," I answered. "It's prob'ly Jonas King. I've sorta been expecting him."

Locks was the head guard of the noon-to-midnight shift. We called him that 'cause he was in charge of locking us in at night. We called the head guard of the midnight-to-noon shift 'Keys' because his crew opened our cells up again in the morning.

"Aye, he's there," Locks said. "But I dunna know the mon wi' him. Claims his name is Br-r-r-annick. Like yours, mon. Jock Br-r-r-annick," Locks volunteered. "Wot d' ye think o' thot, now?" I was jolted clear down to my feet. Jack Brannick? My father?

When I entered the Guest Room I saw Jonas talking to a man I'd never seen before, but whose face was certainly familiar. He looked so much like me it stopped me in the doorway. The man smiled and started toward me, then stopped. He looked as if he'd been about to ask a question and then thought better of it.

"Muddy," Jonas broke the short silence. "This is your father." He paused and looked from me to Dad and back. "We bumped into each other on the street in Cheyenne yesterday. When I told him about you he didn't believe me, at first. But now . . . well . . . here we are." He shifted on his feet. "You two should talk. I have some business with the warden." He left us alone.

My mind was spinning. I plopped onto one of the hard-backed chairs. So this is my Dad, I thought. Dad?! How can I call him Dad? I've never even seen him before. Maybe he's NOT my dad, I thought. That idea was quickly dumped. All I had to do was look at his face. It was my face! With a few lines in it.

Dad started to talk. "I didn't know about you until yesterday when Jonas told me. When I learned that your mother had died I figured I had no reason to come back from Medicine Bow so I just kept moving west."

He talked for quite a while. I hadn't even said hello. I was numb from the neck up. He told me of his travelings. Of working on a California ranch, of dealing poker in a Barbary Coast saloon, of wearing a badge in Sacramento, and finally of shipping out from San Diego and his five years as a seaman.

Then it seemed that it was my turn to talk, but I couldn't think of what to say. Dad asked me if I could remember the Haakens, the family Jonas said had raised me for my first two years. "No, not really. I can sorta remember some folks who sometimes carried me and sometimes walked beside me, but I can't see their faces. I've tried hard."

Well, that got me started, then words and stories just flowed out of me like water. Dad asked a few more questions about the people and families I stayed with and each question would start up another flood of words.

Some of those things were so funny they made us both laugh. Laughing together is almost as good as crying together to break down walls between folks.

Of course, it wasn't all laughs. I told Dad about the worst of my "families," the Clemmettes. "You say it cla-MET," I told him. "They were French. I was about thirteen when I joined them. Mrs. Clemmette and the two little girls were very nice, but Jean Clemmette was a mean, growling slave driver. Everybody called him 'Frenchy.'"

Clemmette was short but very brawny. He had thick black hair on every visible part of his body. "He gave me orders, half in French and half in English. If I ever misunderstood he 'corrected' me with one of his big hairy fists. If I'd have stayed with them for very long I'm sure he'd have killed me. But I got lucky."

I told Dad that Bill King came by one day to check on me. It was the day after one of my 'correctings.' The side of my face was badly bruised. Lud asked what happened to me. I told him.

Clemmette roared that I was lying. "He lies, dat brat kid. No damn good."

Bill's face got red. "This boy doesn't lie, Clemmette. And I'll tell you something else. When I leave here today he's going with me. And I hope you try to stop me."

Unlike most bullies who slap smaller, weaker people around, Clemmette was ready to stand his ground against Bill. With a nasty grin he spread his feet and bent slightly forward. He looked thick as a tree.

"You t'ink you can handle Frenchie, eh?"

I was scared for Bill. Clemmette was at least fifty pounds heavier. But I shouldn't have worried. Bill moved like a cat. He hit Clemmette hard in the chest and sprang back before the hairy man could grab him.

"You should have seen it," I told Dad. "Bill chopped once on each side of Clemmette's thick neck using the edges of his open hands, first the left side then the right, and it was all over! Just that quick! Clemmette was lying on the ground staring at the sky through glassy eyes."

Bill stood over him, fists closed now. "You are going to give this boy a good horse and a fair saddle to pay him for your abuse. I'll pick the horse. Or I'm taking you to jail."

My mouth must have been hanging wide open. There wasn't a visible mark on the squat French brute, but he had clearly lost the battle.

Clemmette's eyes were losing their glazed look as he struggle to his feet. "Da hell I will," he roared. "No good damn kid!"

Bill didn't argue. Instead he said, "You just found out that I can whip you. I can shackle you, too, if I have to. And drag you to court in chains where you'll lose, again. Then you'll go to jail. And I'll see that the boy gets the horse anyway."

Bill paused a moment to let everything penetrate Clemmette's slowly clearing brain. There was no emotion of any kind on Bill's face when he added, "Or you can give him the horse, saddle and a bill of sale right now, and we'll be on our way."

When we rode out of that yard I was bouncing on top of my own saddle, astride my own horse and the bruise on my face didn't hurt any more. The story made Dad laugh.

By the time Jonas came back from the warden's office Dad and me . . . I mean Dad and I . . . had gotten pretty well acquainted (I had a momentary vision, just then, of Miss Mary Lynn Berg of Madison, Wisconsin correcting my grammar and wagging a finger at me).

I explained to Dad how I happened to be "taking my meals" at Larimie Prison for the past three and a half, almost four, years. He got mad, really mad, thinking of Judge Richardson. And Jonas's version of the story didn't make him feel any better. If the judge had been there right then I think Dad would have torn him apart with his bare hands.

Jonas made a point of telling us both that he was making good headway on getting my sentence reversed, or revoked or something.

"The reason I'm so sure that we're going to win is 'cause I told the Territorial Judiciary Council I won't settle for less than a complete revoking of sentence," Jonas said.

"If they give you a parole, you're still a convicted robber – an ex-con. I don't even want you to be pardoned, although I would suggest you take it if one's offered. But getting the sentence dismissed erases it entirely. It's as if it never happened."

To which Dad snorted, "Except for the years . . .years...that an innocent man had to spend in prison just because of a drunken, dishonest fool of a judge." Dad was almost shouting now. He was really mad. Miss Berg would have made me say angry.

"It's long past time that a man like that should have been removed from office. Why hasn't someone taken a shot at him by now? Or are they waiting for an irate father to do it? That's a job I'd apply for." I was enjoying this. My Dad was acting like a dad.

Jonas cautioned him. "The judge is everything you say, and maybe even worse, but a fool he is not! He knows the laws of Wyoming Territory, cover-to-cover, better than anyone else I know of. I have to give him his due on that score," he conceded.

"He's out-foxed me at every turn. And he's suggested to the other judges of the territory that if I get any of his sentences thrown out it will start people looking at their past decisions. They're fairly united on this. That's why I haven't had much luck so far." He didn't paint a pretty picture.

"But I'm gaining,. And there will soon be another territorial judge appointed. I have a strong bit of evidence from the colorful past of the Dishonorable Odell Richardson which I've been saving."

I had kept quiet about as long as I could, so I asked Jonas, "Is it about Mavis Vertin?" I said, remembering the name from the afternoon of the trial.

Jonas's face showed surprise, but Dad was even more so. He asked, "Mavis? What about Mavis?" This time both Jonas and I were surprised.

"You knew her?" Jonas asked Dad. I was mighty curious, too.

"You bet I did. All of us in the mines and gold fields at Medicine Bow knew Mavis." I felt a tightening in my stomach wondering about my mother.

"Several miners had come down with a rash and bad fever. And everybody thought it was smallpox. It wasn't, but folks were scared, so they isolated the sick ones without food or care. Not even food," Dad said.

"Mavis was one of the gals at the 'Pair-o-Dice' saloon. She'd had smallpox and survived. Except for her pock marks she was a very pretty woman. Anyway, when she heard about the fever she came out to the camp and took care of those men. Quite a gal, if you ask me. They called her their 'Angel from Paradise', or from 'Pair-a-dice'."

"I knew about that," Jonas said. "And it was just afterward that the judge tried to get a little amorous with her. When she wouldn't have anything to do with him he beat her up. Pretty badly, too. I talked to Mavis about pressing charges. She said no one would take a dance hall gal's word against a judge's."

Dad said, "I'll bet I know where she could have gotten at least a dozen miners to swear to anything she'd want them to."

CHAPTER 8

Jonas had to get back to Cheyenne, but Dad stayed in Laramie a while. He came to visit as often as they would let him. So often that we soon began to feel like family. It was a good feeling. I was surprised by how easily we always found things to talk about, whether they were serious things or just time-of-day stuff.

After a few days in Laramie Dad went "up the slope" to Medicine Bow, in the higher foothills west of Laramie, to see how the played-out mines looked after nearly twenty years. He stopped back in Laramie to see me on his way down to Cheyenne where Jonas was waiting for him.

Dad was planning to go up to Wheatland and Blainey. He'd never been to Blainey. Said he wanted to see what the place was like where I did most of my growing up. I think what he really wanted was to find the judge.

That's what Jonas thought, too, so when Dad got back to Cheyenne Jonas had a surprise for him. He offered him a job as deputy district marshal.

Strictly speaking, the job was not Jonas's to give but he had been talking to the big boys in the state house about Dad. It was a job that needed to be filled and there were few men in the area who qualified.

It was a federal appointment and it would take at least a week or more to telegraph to Washington, D.C. for approval. Jonas figured that would give Cheyenne time to telegraph Sacramento to check on Dad's record as a California lawman.

Until then it would be a temporary appointment. One that could be erased if Dad didn't pass muster. But more important, in Jonas's eyes, was the fact that Dad would be wearing a badge when he went to Blainey.

The King brothers hoped that would keep him from killing the judge when he found him. Dad accepted. As he later told me, "What the heck, son, I needed a job." He called me son.

A few days after Dad left to go to Blainey I told the men in the cell block about having met my own father. Bojo was especially pleased. This made me think of his parents. They had been killed by the people who raided his village in Africa. I wondered if I should ask him about them and how he came to be in Larimie Prison.

That night in the darkness I did. "Bojo, I'm in here 'cause of a lying judge who hated me. Why are you here? What could a nice guy like you have done to get himself thrown into prison?"

"I killed me a man, Muddy." He spoke quietly into the darkness. "Da man, he grab my Bee-rah. He try to tear her dress off. He hurtin' her. I hit him." He paused a moment then added, "I hit him hard. His neck snap. He dead, so I be here, now."

Another pause, then he said "Bee-rah go somewheres. Do' know where. Maybe she dead. Do' know." I was jolted.

"I'm sorry, Bojo." That was all I could say. "I'm sorry. For all the misery my people have caused you I'm sorry." I remember thinking, *How much can a man be expected to stand? His family, his woman, his whole life gone because some people wanted slaves!*

Things for me were starting to look good. I had found my father! Jonas was closing in on my freedom. My life had just taken a great forward leap. But not for Bojo. I was a long time getting to sleep that night.

The next day brought us a bright, warm morning. I was still happy and smiling about meeting my dad. There was a lot of joking and laughing at noon in the chow hall. I was not ready for the terrible thing that was about to happen.

We were all back on the rock pile, leaning on our sledge handles during our dime time, when we heard someone pass the word, "Krain!".

I spun around and saw him almost upon us. I saw it all in a glance. He was walking fast, his eyes were wild and staring straight at me, his face still showing the signs of Nig's moment of revenge. His right arm was straight, almost stiff looking, down by his side.

He brushed past Nig and reached for me with his left hand. Bojo moved to defend me, raising his arm to block Krain's reach. This was what the maniac was expecting. When Bojo raised his arm he left his chest unprotected.

I saw the shiv, a sharpened piece of steel, appear in Krain's right hand. It dropped from inside his coat sleeve. It wasn't really me he was after. It was Bojo! I didn't realize it quickly enough to do anything about it.

With a grin of madness on his face Krain drove the shiv deep into the center of Bojo's chest. Bojo's huge hands grasped Krain around the neck and lifted him above his head, squeezing.

Krain's legs kicked, his hands beat on Bojo's large arms just twice. Then Nig and I both heard Krain's neck bones crunch. His legs were suddenly still. His eyes bulged and his face was red-purple. He was dead when Bojo released his grip to let him fall.

Then Bojo began to slump. He let himself down to one knee, the shiv still sticking out of his chest, a dirty rag wrapped around the unsharpened "handle" end now coming undone. Bojo sat, then laid down as life was leaving him.

I was finally able to move. I knelt beside him, took his huge hand. "I'm sorry. I'm sorry." I don't know how many times I said it. "I couldn't move, Bojo. I'm sorry."

"Muddy," The big man said, gripping my hand, "I be dyin' now." My eyes were full. Nig was still rooted where he stood, crying, his hands shaking, horror on his face.

"I'm sorry, Bojo," I said again. My mind was over loaded with the awful scene. I could not find words.

"Muddy," Bojo's eyes were not able to see me now. The corners of his mouth tried to smile as his grip on my hand began to fail. "I can read, Muddy. Thank y. . . " His last breath slowly left him.

I stayed beside Bojo until Locks and two other guards moved me to one side, so they could perform their inspection. The warden was called. All the men of the rock pile gang were standing in small clusters, staring. I had plopped down a few feet from Bojo's body.

Warden Schnitger stood a moment looking at Bojo, no readable expression on his face, as usual. Then he ordered Bojo's body taken to the infirmary for burial preparation.

"This vass a goot man," he said in his crisp Prussian accent. "He deserves a funeral. He shall haff one."

All inmate deaths and burials must be recorded and the family, if there is one, notified. Graves are marked without any deference being shown to good or bad, young or old. The only exception might be in how it's done.

"What about Krain, sir?" Locks asked.

"There are some left-over pieces of canvas in the furniture factory," the warden said.. 'Wrap him in one of those."

That's how Krain was buried. Bojo was not buried until a big enough casket could be constructed for him. Warden Schnitger read over him. I was permitted to be there, too.

For the next couple of days all the talk around the prison was about Bojo and Krain. Almost nobody liked Krain, and they all said so. Everybody liked Bojo and they all said that, too. The boys in the cell block asked me to write something about what had happened.

It took me a several days to get going on it, at first. Then I wrote "The Big Man and the Bad Man." I told Bojo's whole tragic story and as much of Krain's as I knew.

The warden asked me not to use Krain's name because some of his family might come around and, if they were anything like Krain himself, they might cause legal trouble. I changed the spelling of Krain's name to Crane. Everyone agreed that it was a good story but no one cheered or applauded

————◆————

I got a new cellmate a few days after we buried Bojo. Curly Wray. I had begun sleeping in the bottom bunk. Bojo's bunk. Most prisoners consider the bottom bunk to be the place of seniority.

Wray, a small-time thief and wife beater, was serving a three year sentence with possible parole after six months. He was about ten years older than me. . uh . . than I (Darn you, Miss Berg) and about the same size. He didn't like the idea that a "kid" of twenty-one was the senior man in the cell so he thought he'd set that straight right away.

When I extended my hand to him he ignored it and snorted, "I'll take the bottom bunk," and started toward it. I deliberately stepped in his way. After more than four years in close confinement with other men I had learned a few things about asserting and accepting, and about doing it quickly. So did Wray, it seemed.

Facing him squarely I said, "Bottom bunk's taken. I'd like to show you something." Without waiting for him to react I grabbed him at the hips with my calloused paws and lifted him up until his head touched the ceiling of our cell, then slowly set him back on his feet.

I think that was the first time I ever felt any pleasure at having done four-plus years of two-ees on the rock pile.

"Now," I said, as soon as I could speak in a normal voice after straining to lift Wray, "We can do this either of two ways. We can fight this fight every day, or we can both just accept that the way things are is the way things are. It's up to you."

The King brothers had taught me to read men's eyes. As Wray turned away, without any comment, I saw in his eyes that he was going to give it one more try.

It's an old trick – turning away from your opponent, letting him think he's won, then suddenly spinning back to catch him in surprise. But I expected it. I was ready and waiting.

Without turning to look, Wray swung his right arm around at shoulder height as he moved in a backward pivot. He expected his fist to connect with my head or neck, but I had gone into a crouch to brace myself.

Wray's fist whooshed over my head and hit the steel frame of the top bunk, breaking one of the bones in his hand. He howled in pain. It would be some time before he'd be able to continue our little dance.

Without further discussion Curly Wray took the top bunk, and the way things were continued to be the way things were. And, broken hand or not, Warden Gustav Schnitger would still expect both of us to be on the rock pile in the morning.

Curly Wray remained sullen and aloof, seldom talking to anyone in our block, preferring the company of one or two convicts of the north wing. I wrote twenty-one more dreadfuls in the next year.

CHAPTER 9

It didn't take long before the monotony of prison routine once again began to blur the passing of time. Since our arrival at "Laramie University" two other men in cell block B had completed their sentences and "graduated." We sent them off with cheers and congratulations. Otherwise, time passed uneventfully.

With the drone of prison life I had forgotten to think about my own "graduation." On a beautiful day in the spring of 1885 I was called into the guest room where Warden Schnitgen and all three smiling King brothers were waiting. I looked around for Dad but he wasn't there. Bill explained that he was up in Casper on an assignment.

Jonas had been successful. I was not paroled. I wasn't even pardoned. My sentence had been revoked! Overturned! Erased! As if it had never happened. But it had happened. And for no good reason.

Dad was right. I had lost six good years out of my life and I was damned mad about it. I mean angry (sorry, Miss Berg). But there wasn't much time spent in being angry just then. I was too excited.

This was Liberation Day! Graduation Day! Freedom Day! I was free to go through those huge front doors walking the other way. Out! But first I had to say my farewells to Nig, Bru, Ted and Pete, and all the other boys in the cell block.

I had been doing some correspondence work and record keeping for the warden over the past six years so when I asked him for permission to get a cake or some candy from the shops in town as my farewell present for the men in cell block B he reluctantly agreed.

Jonas advanced Lud and Bill some of my money, which I would have to pay back as soon as I got to a bank. They rode into downtown Laramie for the goods, which I passed to the boys through the bars after "Locks" had secured them all in their cells for the night.

A piece of frosted cake was something these boys hadn't had since they'd become "guests of the Territory" and they gulped it down, but the real treat for most of them was the fruit.

Somewhere the King boys had found a crate of winesap apples that had been in someone's fruit cellar since last fall. They were starting to wrinkle with age, but the men ate them greedily.

Even Curly Wray. When I passed the cake and apples through his bars the ever-sullen wife beater almost smiled. For just a moment his eyes softened slightly and he said, "Thanks, Muddy," then turned away. He had already moved his bedding down to the bottom bunk.

I don't know if the air really is fresher and better on the outside of prison walls, but it certainly seemed like it. I was so perked-up and happy I could have danced a jig clear across all of Wyoming Territory. But I didn't have to.

Jonas had taken some more of my money and bought a good horse, a fine saddle, a belt gun and holster and a Winchester. I was ridin' high and loaded for bear.

I rode down to Cheyenne along side the King brothers feeling very much in the bosom of my family. The most pleasureful parts of my life had been those times when I had lived with these three men.

Finding Dad was great, but Dad and I hadn't had any life together, yet. Jonas, Lud and Bill had been my "fathers" for most of my life, and now I was riding with all three of them. It was a great day.

Dad had planned to be back in time for my "graduation," Jonas told me, but things hadn't gone as smoothly up in Casper as they had expected so he had to stay a while longer.

It seems while I was in prison somebody had struck oil up there and that started a sort of "gold rush." A lot of rough, tough people came with their marked cards and loaded dice. Dad had his hands full. I would join him there soon.

On our ride from Laramie to Cheyenne Jonas and Bill teased Lud about having a girl. Lud was the shyest of the three brothers, yet it appeared he might be the first one to marry. By now all three were into their thirties.

They kidded Lud on being so bashful that it had taken him all of six years to get to the point of becoming engaged. Or, as Jonas put it, "He pursued her until she caught him." Lud was the only one who didn't laugh at that.

However, Lud was very proud of his bride-to-be and described her to me in great detail. I was quite surprised when he told me that she was a school teacher, tall with blond hair in a bun, that she had come west from Madison, Wisconsin, and that her name was Mary Lynn Berg. I promised Lud that I would be at that wedding no matter where, no matter when.

———◆———

I wanted to get going north to join Dad in Casper, and maybe stop by Blainey on the way, but I needed some walking-around money which was in the bank in Cheyenne. The state of Wyoming did not waste much money outfitting its 'Larimie graduates' in new clothes.

The Cheyenne State Bank was only the second or third bank I'd ever been in. Funny smelling place and quiet as a library. At least, it was until I got there. Jonas introduced me to one of the men inside the cage area and I told him I'd like to take some of my money out.

That teller guy looked at me with a wide grin, then spun around and trotted over to a fat, older man who jumped up out of his black leather desk chair and headed straight for me, a smile on his face and his hand extended.

Pretty soon I was surrounded by all the bank people and several customers, too. They all wanted to meet the man who had written all those "wonderful dreadfuls." I was a celebrity.

I wound up spending most of two days in Cheyenne being slapped on the back and eating free. Can you believe it, I even signed a few autographs! That was the embarrassing part.

Jonas cautioned me, "If you go to Blainey leave the judge alone. I have the goods on him and I'm going use it to take care of him legally. If you decide to go there keep the lid on, Muddy. Don't touch him." I knew better than to mess in Jonas's plans.

Bill King had lawman business in Chugwater, about thirty miles north of Cheyenne, so on the third day of my freedom we rode that far together and shared a room over the saloon that night.

We were just getting our boots off when Charlie Gritt, the local 'roving deputy,' pounded on our door hollerin' for Bill to come help.

It was Charlie's job to keep the peace in Chugwater, Slater, Wheatland, Blainey and all the territory betwixt and between and to telegraph for assistance from Cheyenne when needed.

We had just had supper with Charlie an hour earlier down in the saloon. While we ate he and Bill had finished the business Bill had come there to settle.

Four hard-cases had ridden into town that evening, got the drop on Charlie, took his gun and were now downstairs in the saloon holding someone they planned to rough up a bit and then kill, a man Charlie knew by the name of Carew.

Rather than run two blocks down the street to the jail for another weapon, Charlie came upstairs to get Bill and the extra pistol he knew Bill kept in his saddle bag, then the two of them headed out the door with me right behind them. Bill stopped me.

"Not you, Muddy. This is lawman's work." They left me standing there. Rather than argue I gave them a half minute headstart, then quietly went down the stairs after them. Good thing.

The saloon had a front door for the drinking customers stepping in off the street, and a side door that opened to the small lobby where the hotel customers registered for rooms.

By the time I got down to the lobby Bill and Charlie were standing well apart with pistols drawn, their backs to the front door. They had stopped the four hardcases from beating and kicking Carew, and had ordered them to drop their pistols.

We did not know there was a fifth member of this band. He came through the front door of the saloon carrying a shotgun. He hadn't noticed me standing in the lobby archway. As he raise his shotgun to back-shoot Bill and Charlie I grabbed for my pistol.

What the King brothers had taught me had not been lost, even after six years. My shot took the would-be backshooter in the shoulder slamming him sideways. His load of buckshot went wide. He recovered and tried to use his second barrel on me, but he was too slow.

I knew how to shoot and kill but I'd never had to do it before. I stared at the dead man, stunned. Even after six years living with rapist, robbers and murderers I realized I was not the tough guy I thought I was.

Bill and Charlie fired into the four hoodlums in front of them. Only one of the four men facing them had managed to get off a shot before being downed. Curiously, he was the only one who survived although he did not get off without some damage.

Speaking to the lone survivor, Bill asked, "Mister, you want to tell us about this? Why were you four beating on Carew, here?"

"Carew, hell!" the wounded man snorted. "His name's Harley Beck. He ratted on us to the law down in Colorado. We been trailin' him for near three months." He struggled to prop himself against the bar's footrail.

"I see yuh done fer my partners. Yuh got a couple into me, too, damn yuh."

Charlie said, "You'll be fit to stand your trial and you'll walk into Laramie Prison on your own two feet." Customers were filing back into the saloon. "Some of you boys give us a hand here," he ordered. "Let's get Carew and this jasper over to the jail so we can patch 'em up."

To the bartender he said, "Wilson, get the Chinaman in here to take these bodies out. Tell him I'll be over to check their pockets later. And tell him we'll need four caskets." Deputy Charlie Gritt was a man to have on your side. I already knew Bill was one of the best.

After patching up Carew and the surviving hooligan Bill went through the wanted posters looking for Harley Beck. He found him. Carew, or Beck, was wanted in Colorado for robbery, theft and assault, and for questioning in regard to a murder.

When Carew-Beck was conscious he identified the surviving assailant as a man wanted for at least as many crimes as he himself was. All in all, it wasn't a bad night for law and order.

CHAPTER 10

Next morning we were all up and in the saddle early. Bill had business back in Cheyenne and Charlie was off to Wheatland to see his wife and little girl before making his regular visit to Blainey.

Charlie had told me of a small cafe in Slater, a town just a half dozen or so miles further up the trail, where an old trail drive cook put up a good feed. I figured on having steak and eggs for breakfast that morning.

Slater wasn't much of a town, hardly a wide spot in the road. I was hungry enough to tackle my steak on the hoof, and the smell of griddle cakes and coffee coming out the open door of the Drover's Cafe made it worse. I stepped down and tied up. I wasn't expecting a welcoming committee.

"Well, look who's here. Muddy Brannick, fresh out of prison. Howdy, Muddy." It was Terp Finley, one of the boys from Blainey who used to meet Adorable Dorie in the grove six years back. He was holding down a bench with his backside in front of the cafe.

I remembered Terp as an insolent type, lazy and not too smart, who always traveled with the pack, seldom alone. He used to crowd me with wise remarks about my absent parents. I never did anything about it because he was always with two or more boys just like himself.

He resented the fact that I could read and write, and that the King brothers liked me. The Kings were the heroes of every man and boy in the territory. I got pushed a bit by Terp and his friends.

Today, however, he seemed to want to be friendly. Maybe it was because he was alone, or maybe Terp had changed. We'd both had six years time to do some growing up.

Anyway, he came in and sat with me while I ate my breakfast, not that he helped my digestion much. Didn't matter, though. Steak, eggs and potatoes all fried in bacon grease. Pure heaven.

"If you're headin' to Blainey the shortcut's open now," he advised. "Cuts five miles off the trip. You figger t' go that way?" The shortcut angled out of Slater and led more directly to Blainey than the regular trail did.

I hadn't made up my mind whether to go straight to Casper or drop by Blainey for a quick look-see, first. Terp's suggestion about the shortcut being open made me think about it.

"You say it's open," I asked? "What about Temporary Creek?"

"Dry as a bone," he answered. "Save you five miles. Guess you could make it easy by dark." Then he stood up, put out his hand to shake and said, "I got to be travelin'. I'm ridin' fer the Diamond D now. Got some miles t' get behind me. See you 'round. By the way, nice hat." Until he had made that comment I hadn't noticed that we were wearing nearly identical hats. Mine was newer and cleaner, but it was a twin to his except for the narrow silver band around the crown of mine. Terp had a braided black leather band around his.

Now the cafe was empty except for me and a whiskery-faced teamster who drove the overland dray wagon tied up outside. I settled back for another cup of coffee.

"I'm not s'posed to stop here," he said, making conversation. People who are alone a lot like to visit when they get the chance. "I'm s'posed to go on to Wheatland b'fore stoppin' for lunch, but I know where the eatin's best," he smiled. "B'sides, I'll still make Casper by noon t'morra."

At the mention of Casper I perked up. "Do you know a lawman in Casper by the name of Brannick," I asked?

The teamster grinned again. "I hope t' swear," he sounded almost boastful. "He had to lock me up while back t' keep me from gettin' myself kilt. I got likkered an' was goin' to take on four men, all to once. But Johnny Brannick just stepped in an' waltzed me off t' the hoosegow, an' here I am today, alive an' well an' able to tell of it."

"Well, sir," I said, "John Brannick is my father, and I'd appreciate it if you'd give him a message, if you see him."

"Your pappy? Well, I swan! I surely will. I'll make a point of it. I surely owe him that. What do you want me to tell him?"

"Just tell him that I'm stopping off at Blainey for a day or two before coming to Casper." We finished our coffees, visited a bit more, shook hands and left the cafe.

With my belly full of the best food I'd eaten in six years I rode slowly out of Slater and onto the Blainey short-cut. It was the kind of day you wanted to take slowly. Spring. Warm and sunny. Beautiful.

I heard a meadow lark. That stopped me. A meadowlark! The first one I'd heard in all those six years. Yessir. It was a beautiful day.

I was recognizing old land marks as they came in sight. This added to my enjoyment and made me all the more eager to get . . . I almost said get home. I didn't really have a home. Blainey was just one of several places I had lived. But it was the last one, and the one I had known the longest.

And that right there was another lonesome thought. I really didn't belong anywhere! Just one of many such thoughts I'd been having during my growing up years.

It began to cloud up some. I wondered if winter was going to make one last stand. In an hour large, soft "goose feather" snow flakes were all around me closing off all sounds except those from my horse and me.

The wind began to rise so I got the slicker out of my saddle roll and put it on. It had no warmth, but it protected me from the wet snow and the wind. It was only four or five miles to Blainey from Temporary Creek.

Everybody called it that because it only ran with water during the spring melt. The rest of the year it was just what Terp said – bone dry. When I rounded the small bluff of rock and topped the knoll that led down to the creek I was surprised to see that it was still filled with fast-moving melted run-off. Even with some ice in it.

It appeared that Terp Finley was still pulling jokes on people, and it also appeared that I was still falling for them. This time I got a bit angry, though. This joke had taken me miles out of my way, and I'd have to go several more miles back and around to reach the regular trail.

Either that or wade through deep, fast-moving icy water up to my waist. Not likely. I still had a long ride ahead of me. It would be well after dark before I'd make Blainey.

Stepping down to give the horse a rest I nearly jumped out of my skin when the horn on my new saddle exploded. The snow in the air had muffled the sound of the gunshot. I knew the general direction it had come from but that was about all. As I pulled my rifle out of the boot my horse got skittish and circled so that he got between me and the next bullet. It took him in the head and he fell, pulling me down with him. I almost got pinned underneath him.

I had sense enough to stay down behind the animal's body and wait for the gunman to fire his next shot, but it never came. I waited for close to half an hour before I rose up enough to undo the belly strap and pull the saddle off.

Even though the falling snow made everything white, I still had my bearings and knew just about where I was. And where the shooter was.

To get out of there I had to walk back in the direction of the bushwacker so I held the saddle in front of me as I went. I backtracked over the knoll and around the rocky bluff.

When I figured the sniper was now behind me I switched the saddle around to cover my back. I slipped the Winchester back into the boot and unholstered my pistol.

I was trying to rig the saddle straps like suspenders across my shoulders when I heard a horse coming hell-for-leather up behind me. The rider shot again. His rifle had to have been of heavy caliber 'cause when it struck the saddle it slammed me to my knees.

My first shot missed him as he rode by, but I was pretty sure my second shot scored. In a blink he was out of sight in the heavy snow fall. I had gotten only a glimpse of the horse's rump. The brand looked like a D inside a star. Or was it a diamond?

I got up and started walking. Instead of a five mile walk from Temporary Creek I now had more like twelve miles to Blainey. Pretty soon the snow stopped and after a bit the sun came out and I had my nice day back again.

I saw spots of blood on the grass every so often. If I'd had my horse I'd have tracked my bushwacker. I was still alive but I was not happy.

CHAPTER 11

It took me a couple of hours to get back to the main road where I dropped the saddle and sat down on top of it in the warm sunlight. I didn't rest there long.

A two-horse buckboard came along aimed in the right direction, with a lanky skin-and-bones driver who looked older than the book of Genesis. He had a huge chaw in his cheek and plenty of brown evidence of it showing on his chin. Before I had a chance to ask for a ride he offered one.

"Sorta 'pears yuh've come up short a horse." the old man said. "Th'ow that hunk o' leather into the box an' climb aboard, Sonny."

With a happy grin I said, "Thank you, sir. I surely do appreciate it."

"Not a'tall. Happy fer the comp'ny. Now let's get right to the latest news. What happened to your animal, an' how come yuh to be afoot out here?" He turned away and spat a brown flood.

As I climbed aboard I noticed that the horses pulling the rig both wore what might be the same brand as the shooter's horse. A six-pointed star with a D in the center. I decided to learn a bit more about the lay of the land.

"How about introductions first," I tried. "I'm John Brannick. And how do I address you, sir?" I was sure that Miss Mary Lynn Berg would have been proud of my manners.

"Well now, you are the polite one, ain't yuh," he began. "Hoss Hayes is my handle. I'm head cook and pot scrubber out to the Diamond D spread. I make the best stew in the county, the best apple pie in the Territory and the lightest biscuits in the world, no brag. How 'bout you, Sonny?" I tried not to smile at him, but couldn't help it.

What could I say? I had no job or occupation to speak of. I couldn't very well tell him I can keep prison records, make brooms and furniture, and I'm damn good at breaking rocks. Not hardly.

I finally managed to say, "At present I'm an unemployed writer of western folk lore." Stretching it, but at least partly true. "I'm headed to Blainey for my first visit in several years. But tell me, please, how does one get a name like Hoss?"

He gave me a long appraising look, then said, "My given name is Hoselton, but if I ever hear tell o' you usin' it around I'll take the buggy whip to you."

This time I laughed out loud. "Your secret is safe with me, sir. But, as I sit here looking at the rumps of these horses, I am reminded that I met a Diamond D rider today in Slater." I watched Hoss Hayes for any reaction. "A fella by name of Finley. You know him?"

"Hah!" Hayes snorted. " Got the brain of a colt an' the mouth of a stallion. If the boss's wife told him to shoot the governor, he'd go do it. Damn fool. 'Terp the Twerp' I call him. He a friend of yours?"

"No, sir," I honestly replied. "I don't think I'd care to have him around." Then I asked, "Who's the boss of the Diamond D? I used to travel this area a while back. I don't think I've ever heard of the outfit."

"Used to be the Triangle. Rich fella from back east, name o' Denton, came out here few years back – musta been 'bout a year after you 'went to Laramie' – and bought the place lock, stock an' hired hands. Added a upside down triangle on top o' the first one and made a diamond of it. Not too tough a change. Set his boy Roswell in charge, then couple years later he went back east."

I don't know if I showed it, but he surprised me with his "went to Laramie" remark. How did he know? I decided not to ask just yet.

He continued. "Roswell – we call him Ross – he ain't a bad sort. Got hisself married to the prettiest gal in Wyoming – Judge 'Hizzoner' Odel Richardson's pretty little daughter – an' had a baby . . . all in less than six months." Hoss gave me a knowing glance. "Think o' that now. Youngster's near three or four years old now, I 'magine. Don't 'zactly keep mind o' such things m'self, but that boy, now. He is somethin' fine."

My heart did a spin when he mentioned Judge Richardson's daughter – adorable Dorie – but I was bustin' to ask how he knew about my prison time.

Instead I said, "Is your Roswell Denton a damn fool, or just too trusting?"

"Little bit o' both, I guess. He's smart 'nough 'bout most things 'round the ranch an' such. He's ak-tchally a pretty good rancher. But he's jist purely a damn fool where that wife o' his is concerned. Not that I blame him much," he said grudgingly.

"She's gotta be jist about the mos' beautee-ful female woman I ever did see. Jist seein' her walk across the yard fair makes a man fergit t' breathe. Come near t' gaspin' fer air couple times m'self. Mind yuh now, even at my age." Hoss grinned at me.

"Come t' think on it, she takes that walk most often when the men are in off the range. Kinda likes havin' a audience, she does. When she's riled, though, she gets a frightenin' look in her eyes an' you jist know there's gonna be a tornado." His face took on a hard look.

"The boss'd be well ad-vised to run The Twerp an' a couple others off the place, if yuh ask me. But 'nuff said 'bout that." Hoss shook his head, then he smiled and added,

"That little boy, now. That little Odie. There ain't a man on the place wouldn't go the limit fer him. Me included. Got a smile t' rival the sun. Sorta lights up the place wherever he is, that child."

Our bantering continued until we reached Blainey well after dark, by which time Hoss and I had sized each other up and decided to become friendly. But I still wanted to know more about his "went to Laramie" remark.

"Mr. Hoselton Hayes, in return for the ride, the pleasure of your company, and our good conversation I'd like to treat you to someone else's cooking at the cafe, if it's open this late.

"It is and I do accept, indeed," Hoss smiled his brown-toothed smile. "The Post House Cafe is just yonder. I'll drop you an' your saddle at the door. You can get the first cup o' coffee into yuh whilest I see to these animals, an' I'll join you direc'ly. Ella Finley sets a fine table in there."

That stopped me. "Mrs. Finley? Terp's mother?" I hefted my saddle out of Hoss's rig.

"The very same," Hoss said. "How a fine woman like that could'a hatched such a nothin' egg like the Twerp is b'yond my notion." Hoss slapped the reins and headed for the livery.

I dropped the saddle just inside the cafe door and straightened up to look at the beautiful back of adorable Dorrie sitting at a table in the center of the room. My heart surprised me by skipping, or something. She was still straight, still tall, and still beauiful . I was looking at her back but I'd have recognized her from any angle.

"Well, my gosh. Dorrie! Hello. How are you." She turned to see who I was and I could see that she was now, as Hoss said, a most "bee-yoo-ti-ful" woman. Her head jerked when she recognized me and her smile changed to a mouth-agog look.

She croaked, "My God! Mu. . .Muddy! What. . . uh . . . how . . . are you?" She tried to recover. She was obviously surprised and not at all pleased to see me, 'though I had no idea why. Her eyes took on an angry expression though she forced a smile. "Look, Dad. Uh. It's Muddy Brannick. He's back from. . ."

I hadn't seen the judge sitting there. Six years ago, when Dorrie was in the room she was the only thing I could see. I found it was still like that. It was not easy to take my eyes off her.

I turned to the judge. I was pleased to see he looked terrible. His face was redder than I remembered and his eyes looked worse than his face. They were watery, red-rimmed and painful looking. His nose was wider and puffier than I remembered. And purple, with blotches of red. It looked as if a pin prick would have exploded it.

He had trouble getting to his feet, upsetting his chair as he stood, having to lean on the table. He didn't look at me or say anything, and he certainly didn't offer his hand. He just walked unsteadily past me and out the door. Without another word for me Dorrie followed him. She continued to look angry.

As she passed me I Managed to say, "Dorrie..?" She gave me only a moment's glance. Her beautiful eyes shocked me with the anger and hatred I saw in them. She followed the judge out the door.

Mrs. Finley came from the kitchen, coffee pot in hand. "Muddy!" She gave me a warm welcome. "Never should have happened, you going to prison like that. Never should have happened a'tall."

She led me to a table and poured a cup of coffee for me. She asked me how I was and how I'd been treated during the past six years.

I didn't give her too many details. Just assured her I was glad to be out and didn't want to go back. She put the coffee pot down and sat for a short visit.

There were many things I wanted to ask about: the town, old friends, the new Diamond D, and why Dorrie seemed so angry when I tried to talk to her. She answered all my questions and saved Dorrie for the last.

"That one, now!" Mrs. Finley's face lost its smile. "The beauty of a goddess and a heart of stone. She can turn a July afternoon into a December blizzard with one of her looks. There's only one man in her life and it isn't her husband. It's that beastly father of hers. Cut from the same cloth, those two. There's something funny about the both of them. Seem to feed on each other's hatred."

When Hoss arrived Mrs. Finley jumped to her feet, smoothed her apron and touched her hair. Her smile was back. "Good evening, Hoselton," she smiled. Her voice seemed to smile, too.

"Evenin', Ellie." Hoss gestured in my direction. "Picked up this young fella an' his saddle just north o' Slater. We been jawin' all the way in. Whattaya got fer two hungry loafers?"

Ellie Finley touched her hair again and called, "Krista. Come wait on these two handsome gentlemen while I get things stirring in the kitchen. Bring a cup for Mr. Hayes, dear. Muddy, this is Krista Johannsen, and we couldn't run the place without her."

Krista was blonde, pink-cheeked, freckled and possibly seventeen. She blushed beautifully when I looked at her, but I hadn't quite recovered from seeing adorable Dorrie so I didn't appreciate Krista as much as I'm sure I would have on any other occasion. I did notice she had beautiful eyes.

Her musical voice recited, "Roast beef, a bit well done by this time of day but there's plenty of gravy for it, butter-fried parsnips, this morning's bread, with lots of butter. Oh, and Donelda Simmon's marmelade. I think I can scrape the pan for two helpings of peach cobbler Mrs. Finley made from canned peaches." She stood waiting for our reaction.

"Didn't I tell you Ellie Finley sets a fine table," Hoss bragged. "Works magic in that kitchen. We'll take it all, young lady. Muddy here's buyin'. Say, where'd you find parsnips this time o' year?"

Ellie Finley stepped out of the kitchen smiling proudly. "Root cellar. Last fall's crop. Bit rubbery now, but they fry up just as sweet." With one hand smoothing her apron and the other touching her hair once more she coyly turned back to the kitchen with Krista following.

I told Hoss of my encounter with Dorrie and the judge. Hoss shook his head. "Seen 'em ridin' off down the street in that fancy rig Ross got her. Couldn't get a good look in the dark, but I could tell they weren't smilin'." Hoss was studying my face. "You folks have some words?"

"Well, I tried. I managed to say hello to her and then the two of them left in a scatter of dust, so to speak. Don't ask me why 'cause I don't know. Dorrie I could have visited with. The judge I could have killed."

To change the subject, while we were eating I told Hoss how I came to be afoot. He asked if I had any ideas about who the ambusher might have been, and why. I told him I'd spent the time walking from Temporary Creek to the main road thinking about it.

"Who knew I was back? And who had talked me into taking the shortcut? Terp?! But why?" Hoss made no comment but concentrated on his plate.

We couldn't come up with anything solid that would help clear up the mystery so, after an excellent meal, we went our separate ways. Hoss went on to attend to his own matters. I went looking for my old friend Mick Shane.

I walked into Mick's place and laid the saddle on the bar. The wonderful smells of beer, cigars and spitoons welcomed me back. When Mick saw me he lit up with a great smile that quickly faded. Using only eye movement he signaled me to look around.

CHAPTER 12

Terp Finley was lying across two tables that had been shoved together. A small crowd of drovers surrounded the tables and an older man, with an opened black satchel beside him, was doing a near expert job of cussing while he worked on Terp's wounded leg. It was Doc Feldt, the area's ancient veterinarian.

Doc often did double duty working on both animals and people. Once I watched him sew up a bad cut on Jonas's leg then turn back to castrating calves. I don't believe he even wiped his hands . . . . for either operation.

One or two at a time the drovers began to notice me. One of them must have said something to Terp because he raised up enough to see me. He looked startled. I could barely hear him say, "That's him."

The drovers, all Diamond D men, began to spread out in a line stretching both ways from Terp's tables. Every man had his thumb hooked over his belt, his hand just above the butt of his pistol. It was pretty clear that Terp had told his version of how he got that hole in his leg.

Trying to sound casual I spoke up. "Hello, Terp. I'm surprised to see you again so soon." All eyes swung to look at Terp. I continued,

"Gentlemen, let me introduce myself. My name is Muddy Brannick. Used to live around here when Terp and I were kids." That made them look at Terp again, then back at me.

"Was that before they sent you to prison," a smug, strutting young drover asked in a nasty tone. It was one of the crew that Terp had run around with six years earlier.

"Well, Jimmy Smith. Almost didn't know you without your pimples." Jimmy scowled. Several Diamond D men smirked.

"So you know about my prison time," I replied. "Good." I forced a smile I didn't feel. "I guess everybody 'round here does. And you prob'ly also know the whole story. About the rigged judgement against me and about how that judgment just got overturned, erasing it an' all, so I won't have to go into all of that ." A couple of drovers moved their hands away from their gun butts and onto their belt buckles.

"Right now," I said, "I'd like to talk to you about the backshooter who killed my horse today when he tried to drygulch me. I believe he's right here in this room." I had their attention. This time the drovers' eyes stayed on Terp a little longer.

Jimmy Smith stepped forward, his hand ready to pull his pistol. "I ain't gonna b'lieve nuthin' you got to say, jailbird. I b'lieve you shot Terp from behind an' I'm ready to stand in fer him and settle fer it here an' now."

Mick was holding the old Dragoon pistol he kept under the bar. It had been carelessly pointed at no one in general, but now he pointed it very particularly at the young challenger.

"Smitty, you pull in your horns 'til we hear what Muddy has to say. You so much as twitch your right hand before he's done and I'll make you a new belly button." Smitty looked a little paler, though not much wiser.

"Thanks, Mick," My smile came easier. "One more thing I'll say about myself. I was pretty much raised by the King brothers. I'm sure most of you know of them so you can figure what sort of man they raised me to be. And of course you already know Terp and the kind of man he is. Now, right there you have a fair idea which one of us is tellin' the truth here." Two more drovers hands moved from gun butts to belt buckles.

It only took a couple of minutes to tell the rest of the story, starting with seeing Terp in Slater when he told me that the shortcut was open and Temporary Creek was dry – on that one everybody looked at Terp – to the drygulching attempt at the creek and to my putting a bullet into the drygulcher as he whipped his horse past me in the snow squall. After that the only one with his hand near his gun was Smitty, and he was looking almighty uncertain.

To finish my story I said, "The backshooter put a slug into my saddle, which I was carryin' slung over my back. Slammed me to my knees, saddle and all. Nearly flattened me right out. It had to be a heavy caliber, that rifle." Just about everyone in the barroom again looked at Terp Finley. "Terp, what's the caliber of your rifle?"

When he didn't answer right away one of the older Diamond D riders spoke up. "Terp, here, keeps a Sharps 50." A fifty caliber Sharps rifle is second cousin to a small cannon. Now even Smitty knew the verdict.

I hadn't been in town an hour and here I was already able to send a man to prison. If I wanted to. Even though I knew he had it coming, I didn't want to do it.

"Terp," as I spoke to him he sat up and leaned on one elbow. "It's a known fact that I just got out of prison. I know what it's like in there. I have no desire to send anyone else there unless they're purely bad medicine. You aren't so much bad as you are stupid so I'm gonna give you a choice." He had a snarl written across his face but he was listening.

"You tell me who put you up to the bushwack and why," I tried my best to sound like Jonas. "And you can ride on out of here tonight just as soon as Doc's through patchin' your leg. Otherwise, I make a citizen's arrest and keep you for Charlie Gritt."

"Citizen's arrest, hell." Terp snorted. "You just blew into town from gettin' outta jail. You ain't a citizen of nowhere."

"Who knows," I pretended not to hear his remark that had more than a little truth in it. "Maybe you'll get my old cell. I could even put in a word for you. 'Course, it wouldn't be a good word."

I looked around the room expecting the roof to cave in on me at any minute, but the D riders were waiting for a better choice of options.

One young drover spoke up. "Terp rides for the'D'. He's one of us, ain't he? We can't jes' let some stranger ride in t' town an' point a finger an' us not to do nuthin' about it."

The older drover who had mentioned the caliber of Terp's rifle spoke up. "Oh, I don't know. I'm a 'D' man. I been ridin' for the Diamond longer 'n any of yuh, an' I ain't about to do a thing." This man was a cowboy. The genuine article. He rode for the brand and was loyal to his partners. But those partners were expected to be worth it.

"If Terp's got something to say," he said, " let him say it. I'm willin' to listen. So far I ain't heard him say one thing that makes me want to mix in."

There was some uncertain grumbling among the men but no disagreement. I'd been pretty sure there wouldn't be. No good cowboy likes a backshooter.

"Well, it's sure as hell not all right with me," Doc Feldt straightened up from the table. "Terp's got a broken bone low down in that leg. If he was a horse I'd o' shot the dumb bastard by now." A total stranger listening to Doc could tell in a minute he was no Sunday school teacher. "Once I've put a splint on the damn fool he won't be able to ride anywhere for quite a while."

"Well, Muddy," Terp grinned, triumph sounding in his voice. I decided I didn't like his face when he grinned like that. "Looks like you lose this round. I'll jist mosey on back to the 'D' with the boys. I'll see you sometime." He made an effort to rise.

"You'll sit in jail right here in town 'til deputy Charlie Gritt gets here," I loudly corrected. My turn to grin. "I'm making the charge attempted murder. Your leg will rest and heal just as nicely in the jail as anywhere else."

This caused some more grumbling among the 'D' riders. They were mostly wondering out loud if there wasn't something they were supposed to be doing for Terp. After all, he was a Diamond D man, even though most of them didn't seem to like him.

Mick Shane read the situation and defused it. "It's a fair ride back to the bunkhouse, boys," he volunteered, "so I'll stand the last round before you head out." Two of the older riders grinned and turned for the bar right away. The rest hesitated then followed, and conversation resumed.

Doc Feldt proceeded with the splinting of Terp's bandaged leg and I breathed a bit easier. "We'll keep the leg bound tight 'til morning, then unwrap it to allow for swelling," he said to the barroom crowd. Then to Terp he added, "You're going to have a bad night t'night, I'm afraid."

Thinking back, I could remember seeing Mick's saloon serve as a court room, meeting hall, church and voting booth. Why not as an operating room? It was also the local hotel with rooms upstairs.

When he saw how his old bed sheets were being used Mick complained, "I want all that stuff back, y' know."

Things had settled down. The Diamond riders drank up and left. Doc cleaned up after himself. I stepped out through the batwing doors onto the veranda to see if Terp would be able to negotiate the front steps on his way to the jail.

I didn't know it at that moment but someone was waiting there in the darkness to finish what Terp had tried to do to me at Temporary Creek. I also didn't know that whoever hid there watched me come out, look at the steps, lift my hat, scratch my head, then go back inside. If he'd had his rifle ready he could have shot me right then.

Back inside the saloon Doc said, "Mick, I want you to lend Terp your long handled bung mallet for a cane for tonight. We can fix the dumb bastard a crutch in the morning."

Mick smiled sourly again, "I want that back, too." He wasn't too fond of Terp.

Terp smiled sourly. "Don't worry about it, Mick. Accordin' to everybody here, I ain't goin' no where." He put on his hat – no cowboy goes anywhere without his hat – and hobble-limped to the saloon doors on his splinted leg, leaning on the bung mallet. He paused, sandwiched between the batwings, lifted his hat and scratched his head, just as I had done minutes before.

A rifle flamed from the darkness on the far side of the jail sending a .44 slug through Terp's upraised left wrist smashing his cheek bone, passing through his head and lodging in the door frame. He was thrown against the door frame and back into the saloon onto the floor, very dead. Lamps were blown out and customers dropped to the sawdust covered floor.

No one had seen the flash of the gunshot but I knew where Terp had been standing, and could see where the bullet had struck the door frame. It wasn't too difficult to figure out that the shooter had fired from the direction of the jail. That's where I headed.

Directly across from Mick's was the drug store. As fast as I could, I ran out the doors and across the street, almost turning my ankle in a wagon rut. I ran to the back of the drug store and was cutting left toward the back of the jail when I collided with the shooter in the dark as he headed toward the livery stable.

He was carrying his rifle in both hands, held high. The butt of it struck me on the forehead and fireworks exploded in my brain. Instinctively, I grabbed and held tight on something. Anything! It was the shooter's rifle. As my brain faded into swirling darkness I could hear the shooter's footsteps running away.

I was sure I had blacked out for only a second. When my head cleared I was on my back still holding tightly to the shooter's rifle; my forehead was bleeding. My head throbbed. Mick and a couple of his customers were looking down at me.

"Jeez, Muddy," Mick said, "When you didn't come back we waited maybe ten minutes an' then came lookin' for you. You OK?"

"Ten minutes!" I yelped. Lightning exploded inside my head when I spoke. A little more softly I said, "I've been lying here for ten minutes? Anybody see him? The guy who fired the shot?" No one volunteered anything.

"Ah, hell, Muddy," Mick swore, disgusted with himself. "We waited too long before we dared come out o' the saloon. Whoever it was, he's had time enough t' make it to Chicago by now." He spat on the ground in anger. "I never saw a hair of him."

"Well, I did." It took me a moment to get focused enough to recognize Hoss Hayes's voice. He stepped out of the side door of Johnson's livery stable. "'Least I think I did. Not fer positive, an' I won't say 'til I am, but I'm near most certain who it was. Gimme some time to think on it an' I'll be able to say for certain sure."

Mick got me to my feet and steadied me. We all headed back into the light of the street and on into Mick's saloon, stepping carefully past Terp's body. The pain was blinding at first but got better fast.

Mick brought a towel and a pan of water and wiped my bloody forehead. "Hold this against your head a while to stop the bleeding. It's more of a bump than a wound. I believe you'll live."

Hoss said, "I was some relieved to see it wasn't you that got shot. When I saw the hat on that feller's head I figgered it was all up fer you. Who was it, anyways?"

"The Twerp," Mick answered. "But I think they were after Muddy, here."

"Well, now!" Hoss said. "Well, now! Don't that put a new face on the punkin." Hoss didn't explain that remark and I promised myself I would ask him about it later.

"But who'd want to shoot me?" I asked. " I just got here hardly an hour ago. Nobody even knows I'm in town. Any of you have any ideas? "

"I'd say somebody knows you're here," Mick observed with his usual wry humor.

Hoss chewed his lip a bit. "I'm thinkin' on it. Now you think on this: The Twerp was waitin' for yuh in front o'the ca-fay at Slater. He sends yuh down the wrong road on purpose, an' he's waitin there to 'gulch yuh. Then somebody else ambushes him – maybe cause he's wearin' a hat that looks like yours in the dim light. I'm thinkin' Mick's right. That 'gulcher was after you." Hoss punctuated this with a sharp nod.

Looking at Terp's body still lying just inside the saloon door I tried to change the subject for a moment. "Say, what do you do around here when you have a dead body on your hands? Especially one that's been shot from ambush? Sorta murdered, in fact. And sorta lying around dead on the barroom floor? And it'll be two more days before Deputy Charlie Gritt's due in town."

One of Mick's customers spoke up, a man named Murph. His green plaid mackinaw had seen better days. "We usually send word to the man's kin, if he has any. Else-wise we jest tell whosomever he rode fer t' come collect the body an' clean up the mess, if there is one."

After a thought he added, "Y' know Terp's ma is one of the cookin' ladies over t' the Post House. She's over there now, I b'lieve. B'lieve she maybe owns a piece o' the place. Nice lady. Reckon she heard the shootin'," he took a swallow of his beer and wiped the foam off his whiskery lip. "Who's gonna tell her 'bout this?"

Mick nodded in agreement. "You're right, Murph. She's a very nice lady. I'll go on over." He paused to think for a moment, then said, "Murph, how about gettin' behind the bar 'til I get back. You can give each of your three pals a short beer after they scoot Terp's body to the side of the door and cover it."

To one of the three friends Mick said, "Stan, I want you walk on down to my place and tell my missus what's happened here, an' tell her to get one or two other ladies and come sit up with Miz Finley. She'll be wanting company. Then stop by the livery and tell Johnson to come take Terp out of here. Murph will pour you your choice when you get back."

I was quite impressed with Mick's efficiency and said so. "Mick, I'd guess this is not the first time you've had to handle a situation like this. You're a one-man township board and tornado."

Mick grinned at me. "Got to be. I didn't tell you . . . I'm also the mayor now. Wouldn't do to have dead bodies clutterin' up my place of business." The grin was a mile wide when he walked out through the swinging doors to go attend to his grim business.

I called after him, "Mayor? Are you kidding?" I could hear him laugh as I joined Hoss at the bar. "Hoss, whose rifle is this?" I was still holding the weapon I had gripped so tightly that the shooter couldn't tear it from my unconscious hands.

CHAPTER 13

Hoss squinted a bit. "Now don't you go jumpin' to no con-coosions, young fella, but I know that weapon. An' I know who owns it." There was reluctance in his voice. "I know one thing more, too. He wasn't the shooter." Hoss had my complete but impatient attention.

"Well?"

"Well, . . .," Hoss clearly didn't want to say what he had to say. "That there's a short-barreled, breech loadin' carbine such as the cavalry used a few years back. Easy t' handle an' reload from the deck of a fast movin' horse. Real accurate within couple hun'rd yards,"

"I don't want to buy it, Hoss. I just want to know who owns it." I was getting excited. "And how do you know this owner didn't do the shooting?"

"Aw-right," Hoss's resistance crumbled. "This here rifle b'longs to my boss, Roswell Denton. He cut his initials on the butt, there. See 'em? Watched him do it. But he didn't pull the trigger."

"How can you be so sure, Hoss?"

"Lots o' reasons," Hoss answered. "Fer openers, He ain't the type t' do a job like this. Next, he's a big man, Ross is. Tall as you an' heavier. Fella who ran into you was lots shorter an' smaller. Also, if Ross

Denton had tried to yank that rifle out o' your hands he'd o' done it, an' you along with it," Hoss smiled at the thought.

"'Nother thing," Hoss was uncomfortable again. "The shooter sure didn't run like no man I ever seen. Sorta had a dancin' like way o' runnin'."

A bit surprised, I said, "Wait a minute! You're saying that the shooter was after me. And that the shooter was a woman. I don't know any women around. . . . Holy . . .!"

Reading the expression on my face Hoss said, "Now you're thinkin' aintcha?"

I almost yelled, "You don't mean it was Dorrie? Adorable Dorrie? The "honorable" Odell Richardson's darling daughter? Ross Denton's own wife?" My voice climbed a notch as I realized and spoke each part of the remark.

"Didn't say that," Hoss objected. "I said it was somebody small who ran sorta woman-ish like an' wasn't strong enough to yank that rifle out o' your hands. Didn't say who it was."

"But that's who you think it was, right?" I asked.

The old cowboy rubbed his tobaccoy chin and in a subdued voice said. "'Fraid so. Yep. That's who I think it was." He scuffed his feet in the sawdust. "You hear what I just said?" his voice came back strong. "I said I think that's who done it. Not certain sure."

"Well, Hoss. As you said, that does put a new face on the punkin. Let's look this whole thing over." I began to review everything aloud, more to make it clearer to myself than for any other reason. My head was still aching, my brain a little fuzzy.

"I got out of prison four days ago. I'd have been here two days ago if I hadn't stayed those extra days in Cheyenne. When I got to Slater there's Terp waiting for me. He gets me to take the shortcut so he can dry gulch me, but he didn't do so well on that. Then he gets ambushed 'cause he's wearing the same kind of hat as I was. And it appears that the shooter might have been his boss, adorable Dorrie. That about how it reads to you, Hoss?"

"'Pears so," Hoss agreed, unhappiness ringing in his voice.

"So it also appears that someone who knew that I was out of prison, who also knew that I would be coming this way, who knew I had stayed two days in Cheyenne – which is just about impossible, 'cause even I didn't know I'd be staying – this same someone told Terp when and where to watch for me." I paused a long moment before adding,

"There's a lot of 'whos' and 'maybes' in that figuring," I said. "And here's one more. It also figures to be the person who told Terp to shoot me. And you think it's Dorrie."

"Sorta shapes up that way, don't it?"

"Y'know, Hoss," I scratched my head. "I'm twenty-three years old and I've never tasted hard liquor. But I think right now I could use a drink."

Hoss grinned and turned to Murph, behind the bar, "Give both of us a touch o' the good stuff Mitch keeps hid next t' that old Dragoon pistol."

Murph filled two shot glasses from a labeled bottle and pushed them across the bar. I took my first sip of hard liquor. It tasted terrible, stung my tongue, made my eyes water and burned all the way down. If Hoss hadn't been watching I'd have spit it out. I managed to choke it down and croak out, "This is the good stuff? Gaaah! And I thought beer was bad."

Hoss laughed. I managed a smile, too, as I wiped water from my eyes. "Hoss, there's still something wrong here," I reasoned. "Dorrie has no reason to hate me. The only thing she could blame me for is for being too stupid to realize what she was offering me six years ago. But that's no reason to kill me. It's got to be something else. Or someone else."

"Wondered how long it'd take yuh t' come 'round to that," Hoss said. "You ain't a'tall as dumb as yuh look." Grinning he gestured toward one of the green-topped tables. "Let's sit."

Hoss sat facing me. My back was toward the swinging doors. He said, "You had time yet t' wonder how I come t' be out on the Slater road? How come I friendlied up with yuh so quick an' easy?"

That surprised me. In spite of having spent the last six years of my life with thieves and murderers, it had not accurred to me to be the least bit suspicious of Hoss. It seemed I was still naive and wet behind the ears.

"Fact is," Hoss went on, "I knew who yuh was when I first seen yuh sittin' on yer busted saddle a-side the road 'twixt Slater 'n' here this afternoon. Yuh look jist about how yuh did six years ago, 'cept maybe a bit older an' heavier an' fuller. Been sorta watchin' for yuh." Now that really surprised me, but before I could say anything he asked, "Don't that put a question or two into yer head?"

"Not more than a hundred or so, I'm sure," I answered. "OK. How did you happen to be on the road today? And why did you "friendly up" so easily? And who shot Terp? And who put him up to the bushwack in the first place?" A lot of questions, and I wasn't done yet.

"And who knew when I was to get out of prison? And who told Terp that I would be two days late getting to Slater? For that matter, how could anyone have known that when I didn't even know it myself until it happened."

Then, realizing what Hoss had just told me I said, "Wait a minute! You knew me six years ago? I'm embarrassed to say I don't remember you, and you're not someone I'd likely forget ".

"Well, don't strain yer mem'ry on it," Hoss drawled. "You didn't know me back then, and I didn't really know you, neither, but I sat in on ever' minute of that trial o' yers. Best show in town," he chuckled.

"I was there when the judge 'sent yuh up the river' on that bum rap. Man, that was somethin'." Hoss frowned and shook his head. "The judge lost hisself a lot of respect over that. An' you won yerself a whole lot of friends, me bein' one of 'em, not that it ever done you much good so far."

"Well," I said, "At least that explains how you knew me when you saw me back there on the road, but it doesn't tell me how you knew when I'd be there. What about that?"

Hoss gave me a half disgusted can't-you-figure-anything look and replied, "I aw-ready tol' yuh that I'm the cook on the D spread. Most ever'body on the place is in my kitchen, one time or 'nother, havin' coffee an' sinkers an' such. An' everybody talks." He paused to let that sink in.

"Sometimes it's jist the judge an' Dorrie – an' me. Sometimes folks forget I'm there a'tall. An' sometimes they talk right out 'bout things I got no business knowin'. Sometimes I jist per-tend I'm deef an' blind. But I ain't." He was smiling again.

Hoss seemed to be having a good time making a short story a lot longer, so I just let him take his time. I was learning. I figured he'd eventually get around to telling me whatever it was that he wanted me to know.

"'Pears as how the judge has a friend in the bank where you got yer money stashed," Hoss observed. "All that money you got from writin' them stories o' yers whilst in prison. An' he knows, to the penny, how much yuh got." He winked.

"Also 'pears like that friend has been sendin' the judge a letter or a telee-gram, time to time, tellin' of yer progress. Neat, huh? An' speakin; o' friends, don't you sell "Hiz Honor" short. There's lot o' folks owe him for deals he's helped them with. An' he knows how to collect."

I didn't quite believe my own reasoning. "Now everything is starting t' point to the judge. But what reason has he to hate me? Fact is, I should hate him. Come to think of it, I do. A lot."

"Oh he hates yuh, awright," Hoss said. "An' so does Dorrie,I seen her face change t' somethin' scary when her an' her daddy git talkin'. Them two are a pair o' rags tore from the same quilt. Whoever her daddy hates, she hates! I think they're both a little loco." He shook his head again.

"An' lemme tell yuh about the judge. He didn't quit drinkin' after sendin' you t' prison, y' know. Not by a damn sight, he didn't. Right now him an' his liver are six years drunker an' sicker than the last time you seen him." It seemed to please Hoss to say it.

"An' Mister Jonas King, 'ttorney-at-law, has kept rilin' up the waters 'round your sentence 'til he got the thing wiped off the books. Turnt around! Ree-voked. Or whatever. Now the judge hates Jonas an' you. An' anybody connected to you two. That includes Jonas King's two depity brothers. An' you know what that tells yuh about dear, darlin' Dorrie's feelin's."

Suddenly Hoss's eyes widened. He yelled, "Down!" and threw himself to one side. I started to turn when the lights went out. My lights. I went swirling down into blackness.

CHAPTER 14

I was swimming in Temporary Creek. The water was cold and very thick. I could hardly make any headway fighting the current. Ice chunks bumped into me as they sped by, but I hardly felt them. Looking down into the stream all I could see was darkness, and the thick water was pulling me down. I tried not to let my head go under. I was afraid I wouldn't be able to get back up. I was afraid.

Bojo was trying to reach me from the creek bank. Krain was on the creek bank, too. He had his shiv. I tried to yell to Bojo to look out but I slipped under the surface of the thick, black water. I went down. Way down. Then I felt myself coming up. The water seemed brighter and warmer.

My feet touched bottom and I could stand. Soon I was able to walk in the water which wasn't thick or dark anymore. I waded toward the creek bank. Bojo and Krain were gone. The water was disappearing as I walked. And I could hear voices. I tried to open my eyes.

Doc Feldt was swearing. "Dammit, Muddy! What the hell are you doing being awake? For that matter, what the by-god hell are you doing even being alive?" he snorted at me. I had expected to look up from Mick's sawdusty floor and see Hoss. Instead, I was lying on my side in a bed.

We were in one of Mick's rooms above the saloon. Doc Feldt was doing something awfully painful to the back of my head while he colored the air with his marvelous four-letter-word vocabulary. Doc's bedside manner was not meant for ladies.

"You've got a damn hole in the back corner of your head the size of a half dollar where you lost a piece of your skull."

This time my head really hurt. Twice in one night was too much. Running into that rifle butt was painful, but it was nothing like this. I was pretty sure I was going to regret it, but I decided to try again to open my eyes. I was right. It hurt like hell!

Doc continued. "I took a helluva lot of wood splinters out of your back, and a small piece of lead out of the back of your head. The bullet broke up a bit going through the back of your chair and most of it was deflected up and almost missed when you turned your head. Notice I said almost. If you were a horse. . . . ." Doc's favorite remark.

"Well now, I'm certainly glad to hear all that," I said, trying to sound funny. "'cause I'd be mighty disappointed if all this pain in my head was for some little thing like gettin' kicked by a Clydesdale. Wait a minute." I just realized what Doc had said. "Bullet? What bullet?" I jerked and sparks exploded in front of my eyes.

"Gawdammit, Muddy! Will you shut up long enough for me to finish my damage report," Doc snorted. Then he said, "Wait a minute," changing subjects. "Where the hell did you ever learn about Clydesdales? They're Scottish horses. I don't think there's a half dozen of them in the whole United States."

Without waiting for an answer he jumped back to his report. "Anyway, that piece out of your skull was hanging on to your head by a thread of skin. I just laid it back in place slick as y' please," he smiled smuggly. "Wrapped one of Mick's cleaner towels around your head. You're going to heal just fine – along with a rip-roaring infection and one helluva headache."

"OK, so I got hit from behind by a bullet. What bullet? Who shot me? And why? Tell me what happened? Ow, ow . . . ow!" Saying all that made my head hurt so much I couldn't see for a moment.

I looked around the not-so-roomy room where I lay and saw that Dad was there. So were Lud and Bill King, Hoss Hayes and deputy Charlie Gritt. "If Jonas were here," I managed to smile as I winced, "We'd have a full house."

"I don't know," Doc observed. "This place appears to be a bit over full as it is."

"Sorry Doc. I meant a good poker hand. Three Kings and Dad and me – a pair of Jacks. That's a full house." I thought that was a clever observation. "Kings full over jacks." Nobody laughed "Well, isn't anybody going to tell me what happened?"

Hoss spoke up. "B'lieve that's my department since I'm the only one who seen it all. It was the judge 'at did it." That surprised me so much that I tried to sit up and was rewarded by another kick from the Clydesdale. Pain shot through my head like more lightning.

"That bloated, red-faced bastard," Hoss fumed. "He poked his purple nose over Mick's batwings and aimed his shiny new, nickel-plated Smith and Wesson at us. He was shakin' so bad I wasn't sure which one of us he was aimin' at so I just yelled 'Duck', an' I got!"

"We still aren't sure who he was after," Charlie offered. "We know that the judge hates you, Muddy, and all three King brothers. We also think he might have figured out that Hoss overheard too much in the Diamond D kitchen. We're not sure. But we think it might be dangerous for Hoss to go back out there now. Besides, Hoss is our only eye witness to the shooting."

"Our star witness, you might say," Bill King added.

Dad had been quiet until now, but fatherly concern got the best of him and he asked, "Muddy, You all right, son?"

I was still getting used to having a father and all the things that went with it. I'd been called "son" by any number of older people over the years, but when Dad said it I felt a little lift. It made me smile.

"I'm fine, Dad." And calling him 'Dad' gave me another little boost. "But, to quote Doc, I've got one helluva headache."

Doc rejoined the conversation. "Muddy, I don't want you lying on your back for a while. I did a little patch work back there but that's not the real reason. It's not good for that head wound of yours, even though I got it pretty well wrapped. Sleep on your side. And stay in bed 'til you can scamper through the pasture without it hurting."

He grinned at everybody and added, "Same advice I give all my four-legged patients." Then to me he added, "You've been lying still for three days. That's good. I figure two or three more should do it."

"Three days!" I yelled, and the Clydesdale kicked me in the head again. A little more quietly I added, "I've been lying here for three days?" Even that hurt. "Well, what's been done about the judge," I asked even more quietly? "Is he in jail? Boy, I want to see that."

"So far we haven't done anything about him," Bill said. "Jonas told us to keep the lid on things 'til he gets here. Jonas is in court in Cheyenne, but he'll be here in a few days. We've had a time, though, keeping your dad from doing our work for us. He'd like to show the judge a little 'appreciation' for the way he treated you six years ago, not to mention trying to kill you the other night." Everyone smiled at that.

"Jonas says he has all the ammunition he needs to put that wheezing booze bag into 'Larimie University' legally," Lud added. "Maybe he'll get your old bunk, Muddy." I had to smile at that, even though that hurt, too.

———◆———

Three days is a long time to be cooped up in a room not much bigger than my old prison cell. I wasn't short of company with Dad, Bill, Lud, Charlie Gritt and Hoss visiting, but I began to feel caged. Mick brought me meals so I didn't even get out to eat.

Finally, by suppertime of the second day I'd had enough. I informed them that I was heading for the Post House Cafe for supper.

"I'm not surprised," Dad commented. "There's a freckle-faced beauty named Krista who's been asking about you every time we show up there."

Although I liked hearing that, I pretended not to. Instead I said, "If you'd care to join me I'll buy." I buckled on my gun and headed for the door.

"Well I should hope you would," Lud joshed, coming along behind me. "You've got all that money stashed in that Cheyenne bank and here you are walking with three of the poorest paid public servants in the territory. You know how little they pay us deputies."

"Don't listen to him, Muddy," Charlie laughed. "Lud's still got the first dollar he ever earned. Never spends a cent when he can get someone else to buy." That made Lud's ears a little red but he smiled at the friendly attack.

"You're smart to save your wages, Lud." I sided with him. "If you're going to marry my favorite teacher, Miss Mary Lynn Berg, I expect you're getting ready to set up housekeepping in a nice rose-covered cottage, and I hear they cost money."

We all continued to kid Lud as we headed down the street, and they kept asking me about Krista Johanessen. This kept me from noticing what they were really paying attention to – the large number of loafing cowboys we were passing.

Chapter 15

Inside the Post House we were surprised to see Hoss, in a very clean apron and no tobacco juice on his face, clearing dishes off tables.

"Got tired o' layin' around doin' nuthin'," he explained. "So I thought I'd help the ladies out a bit. The food's good here and the apple pie is spectac'ler. Figger you might guess who baked that pie."

Dad took charge of the seating arrangements, which surprised me. He sat me with my back to the door, a position I had recently come to dislike. He sat facing me at the other end of the table, with Bill and Lud on one side and Charlie on the other. He explained it all.

"Those loafers we saw on our way here, I saw a couple of them in Casper. They're 'fast buck - no work' boys. Gun-for-hire types. They were looking us over a little too closely to be casual. Muddy, if they come through the door after us the four of us will stand. You stay low so you don't catch one of our slugs."

"Well that's just the sort of thing to help a fella's digestion," I answered.

Krista, smiling and blushing, brought us coffee and took our orders for food. Dad was right. She did have freckles. And nice eyes.

And Hoss was right about the food. It was good. And his pie was "spec-tac'ler." After we had eaten he joined us and enjoyed our compliments while we drank our coffee. I was the restless one so the 'big question' came from me.

"Is there a plan for getting the judge?" I asked. "Jonas or no Jonas, from what you're telling me, we'll need a plan of some kind if they start something. Even I can see that."

"You trying to tell the lawmen how to tend to the law, young-ster?" Dad said it a bit sternly I thought. This time it was my ears that were red. "But Muddy has a point," he told the others. "If they bring this hog-rassle to a head before Jonas gets here, we'd better be ready." Bill nodded his agreement.

Hoss leaned forward to get into the conversation. "There's some strangers in town, all right, but a couple o' them boys in the street are friends o' mine from the D. They tell me somethin's up out at the ranch," he reported.

"Seems young Ross has took his son for a vacation trip to Cheyenne for a week or so. Little Miss Dorrie was s'posed to go too, but she pretended to come up lame an' stayed home, keepin' close t' Daddy. In the meanst while, seems the judge has hired hisself a few special hands. They all got well oiled guns and don't know nuthin' about cattle."

"So," I said, "Adorable Dorrie stayed home with Papa, and Papa has hired himself a few 'special deputies' of his own, eh?"

"So I'm told," Hoss said. "An' the fu-ther word from my pals is that her an' her pappy are hell-bent on doin' in just about ever'body who's right now sittin' at this table." He looked around the table in mock concern. "'Pears I'm gonna have to be more select-ful in the comp'ny I keep," he joshed.

Movement behind Dad caught my eye. A large man whose face hadn't seen soap or razor in a while was standing in the kitchen door-way drawing his pistol. Then several things happened at once.

Dad yelled, "Down, Muddy!" He and the others stood, drew and fired over my head at two men who had rushed in the front door of the cafe. I leaned to the right and fired past Dad's left hip, putting two slugs into the man in the kitchen doorway. I don't even remember drawing my colt.

The two men at the front of the cafe had tried to rush through the door at the same time, sideways, with pistols drawn. Later, Lud said it was only the fact that they had to straighten around to shoot that prevented them from scoring a hit.

All three attackers were carried out of the Post House weighing just a few lead ounces more than when they'd walked in.

The other supper customers had the good sense to put their hands up and back into the far wall so we wouldn't think they were part of the action.

As Charlie Gritt rose to shoot he knocked Hoss backwards off his chair and onto the floor. "Well, now!" Hoss sputtered. "Well, now! I b'lieve I'd ruther do without the after-dinner entertainment nex' time, gents. Jes' coffee fer me."

I was beginning to feel that I was stretching my luck a bit thin. First the dry gulching at Temporary Creek; then the ambush that got Terp killed; third the judge's shaky pistol shot in Mick's saloon; and now number four in Mrs. Finley's cafe. And my headache was trying to kill me, too.

The opening shots had been fired. Our war had begun. We suspected our three attackers were working for the judge but even Hoss didn't know who they were. It was clear that they were after one or all of us. We decided we'd better stick together. Never travel alone. Sleep in a safe place. We decided to headquarter in the jail.

In the jail office there were four small windows about ten inches square, one in each of the side walls and one on each side of the front door. They provided a pretty good view of the street. Also, there were two bunks in each cell, and a couch in the office. Accomodations for five.

Hoss announced, "Don't make no space fer me. I'm sleepin' in Johnson's loft. Don't seem natur'l fer a man to be in jail 'less he has to. What's more, I'm prone to roam about some at night. Need more room. B'sides, I'll be up a bit early helpin' the ladies at the ca-fay git breakfast ready".

I took the old leather couch in the office. My head wound ached enough to keep waking me up. I figured the snoring racket of the others and my head would probably keep me awake most of the night.

Sometime after midnight, while trying to walk off another headache, I looked out through those four windows and observed that the only building with a light burning at this late hour was Mick's saloon. There were a few lanterns hanging on posts along the street, otherwise the street was dark.

I was thinking of Bojo just then. And of a trip to the rock quarry taking supplies to the blasters. Just the two of us – trustees – and only one guard.

We watched a "powder monkey" set his dynamite charges in holes drilled into the rock. He attached the fuses, then backed away to a safe distance before lighting them, uncoiling the spools of fuse line as he went.

We watched the blue-black plumes of fire and smoke hiss and swish their way up the quarry wall and enter the charged holes like flickertail gophers. Seconds later the wall exploded. A sight, a sound and a smell I'll probably never forget.

I was startled out of my memory by the smell. The smell of the burning fuse! It was right below the window where I stood. I hollered, "Everybody up!" and in my stocking feet I ran out the door and around to that side of the jail.

There were still four or five feet of fuse left to burn before it would reach the four sticks of explosive. Plenty of time. I grabbed up the sticks, yanked the fuse and tossed it, leaving it to burn itself out. I spun on my heels and and ran back into the jail as damn fast as I could, powder sticks and all, expecting to feel a bullet at each step.

Whoever was watching from the darkness across the street was probably expecting an explosion and not some guy in stocking feet. He only got off one shot.

It was almost a good one, too. It splatted into the plank wall where my head had just been. The shooter knew his business. And my luck was still holding.

I slammed the heavy door shut and dropped the two-by-four bars into place as two more bullets hit the door. Dad and the others were into their boots by now and rushing to see if I was in danger.

"This was for us." I showed them the dynamite. "Too bad to spoil their fun." Then I cautioned them, "No point in trying to go out that door," I said. "They've got a man across the street who can hit what he shoots at. Looks like we're in here for a while."

Charlie Gritt laughed. "Oh, yeah, I forgot. You've been away. Well, while you were taking your meals in Laramie we've been diggin' a back way out of here."

"Three or four years ago," Bill added, "We put our county 'hard labor' prisoners to work digging a trench. Now it's a covered tunnel and it comes up inside the barn in back of us. Most people don't remember it or ever even knew about it. Let's get out of here."

He led us back into the hallway between the two cells. Lud pulled up a section of the floor and dropped through the opening. We all followed carrying our rifles and pistols.

In the darkness of the barn Lud gave us our orders. "Separate, but stay close enough to call to the nearest man with a strong whisper. Hold your fire unless forced to shoot. Try to get across the street and behind a building without being seen." I was still pulling my boots on and my head ached like hell.

'We'll re-group behind Mick's," Lud continued. "and decide on a plan when we've seen what's what. Remember," he reminded us, "We're still trying to 'keep the lid on' 'til Jonas gets here – if that's possible."

CHAPTER 16

No one wanted to rush directly across the street toward the bank. We were all sure the unseen rifleman was waiting there for us.

I walked on soft grass from the back of the jail to the darkness beside the drug store.

For a long two minutes I stayed in the store's shadow, then crouching low and walking on the toes of my boots I started across the street toward Mick's front door.

My rifle friend had moved, too. Now he stepped from the shadows beside Mick's. Even in the dimness I could see the white of his shirt where his vest was open. "Well, look-a-here," he gloated lifting his rifle.

I couldn't see his face but I could almost feel him smiling. My pistol was in its holster and my rifle was pointing the wrong way. I was dead meat.

I heard the shot but felt nothing. Then I realized the rifleman had been slammed back against the saloon wall. I heard Hoss's hoarse whisper from the loft door of the livery, "Watch yerse'f, youngster. An' git the hell outa thuh street, dammit."

I was across the street and into the darkness alongside the saloon in a second. I had to step over the dead rifleman. The hole from Hoss's bullet was leaking a dark stain on his white shirt.

I've heard that a cat has nine lives. This was number five for me. Six if you count the dynamite that didn't get to explode. My luck was too good to last.

Looking through a murky, fly-specked window on the side of the saloon I saw they had Mick. He'd been stripped to the waist and was sitting on a chair with his hands tied behind him. Several men were watching a burly, unshaven man threaten Mick with his knife.

Mick's chest and face were already bloody from several short scratches and cuts made by the knife, and it looked as if the big man was going do more.

I wasn't sure what I was going to do, but I had to do something. My pistol was half way out of the holster when a quiet voice from behind stopped me. A voice I knew.

"Freeze, Muddy," the soft voice said. I could hardly believe I was hearing it. "Turn around slow. An' leave your pistol in the holster." As cautiously as I could, I turned to face my old cell mate, Curly Wray, his steady pistol only inches from my face.

"Damn, Curly," I managed to say. I was shaking. Less than a minute ago I was about to be gunned in the street, now here I was facing a six-shooter in the hand of a man I never got to like. "What are you doing here? Break jail?" I knew that last question was stupid.

I corrected myself. "No. No one gets out of rock knocking school unless Warden Gus himself opens the door for you. So how'd you do it?" I tried to sound calm and make conversation while I worked at getting my shaking under control.

Curly chuckled. "Just like you said." The light from the dirty window was enough for me to see him smile. "My three-year sentence got cut to one. Warden 'Gus' shook my hand and showed me the door. Hell, if you'd waited a week I coulda rode up here with you." He chuckled again.

If what he said had surprised me, what he did next almost bowled me over. He holstered his pistol! How do you figure it? I'm standing there still holding my rifle, and he puts his pistol away. We just looked at each other for a few seconds before he spoke again.

"Muddy, I was hopin' you wouldn't be here when I got here. When I hired on to do the judge's dirty work I already knew about you an' him. How he sent yuh up river fer no good reason." Curly's face was yellow-orange in the window light.

"I figger I owe yuh, Muddy. Back in Laramie you were always square, no matter how I was. This might su'prise yuh, but I'm a man as pays his debts, an' I figger I owe yuh. So here it is. I ain't gonna plug yuh. I figger this makes us even." He even smiled.

"Don't get foolish an' think I grew a conscience. I ain't. I'm still workin' fer the judge. I owe him, too. The next time I see you I'll be shootin'. Just so you know." He turned and walked away from the light. He wasn't the least bit worried that I might cut him down from behind.

Alone again, I was standing exposed in the light from the barroom window. I moved to the back door, even though I knew Mick seldom forgot to bar it. It wouldn't budge. The sloping cellar door was just a few feet to the side. It was unlocked.

I was supposed to rendezvous with the others but they weren't here yet, and Mick's situation was a bit more immediate. I found the narrow steps by reaching into the black pit with my foot. I felt my way across the cellar floor to the ladder and climbed up and through the trapdoor.

I didn't know how many men I would be facing, nor exactly where they were sitting or standing. Peering through cracks in Mick's shot up old mahogany bar I located four men and Mick's burly tormenter. Five in all. I stood up, pistol in my right hand, and spoke loudly.

"Everybody just stand easy." All heads swung toward me. "Don't touch your guns. Just unbuckle and drop 'em." My heart had a hammer inside it that kept time with the throb in my head. I rested the heel of my gun hand on the bar so no one could see it shake.

My count was wrong! There were six men! The sixth was a red bearded man to my right at the end of the bar where the mahogany must have been good. I hadn't seen him. Without turning I could see he had me covered with his pistol. Time for me to be worried, again.

His voice was calm, which worried me even more. "Just lay your piece on the bar 'til we git this thing sorted out a bit, neighbor," he said softly. "Push it away from yuh an' tell us who yuh are and what's your part in all this."

My hopes lifted just a bit. They didn't know who I was. I was sure they'd kill me as soon as they figured it out.

I let my body relax and my head slouch down as if in defeat, and leaned forward until my body touched the bar. This kept my left hand out of sight of Redbeard. I felt beneath the bar for Mitch's Dragoon pistol as I made a slow showy display of sliding my own pistol down the bar toward Redbeard.

Redbeard turned slightly in the direction of the burly knife wielder. "Stick," he called. "What yuh wanna do with him?"

The man with the knife kept his back to us and his attention on Mick. Redbeard caught my movement when I leaned back to bring up the Dragoon, but he turned back a bit late.

I fired the heavy pistol into his face. The soft lead slug snapped his head back as it entered, and spread the back of his skull over the wall behind him, throwing him backwards onto the floor. I'd have puked right there if I hadn't had other things on my mind just then.

Grabbing my own pistol off the bar I faced them again, this time with a weapon in each hand. "Gentlemen," I hoped my voice was steadier than my knees. "I believe you were about to unbuckle and drop 'em," I was feeling good again. "Let's get to it, shall we?"

They looked at Stick, their leader. His body slowly tensed. Just looking at the back of his head it was easy to read that he was going to make a foolish, face-saving move. The others were waiting to see what it would be. I was afraid they would follow his lead.

"Stick," I spoke loudly calling him by the name Redbeard had used. "You're thinking of trying your luck. Understand this: Any man with a weapon who moves . . . any man . . . dies. In fact, any man who does not unbuckle right now. . . dies. Stick, you'll be the first. Do it now!"

That broke the moment. Gunbelts thudded on the sawdust-covered, spit-spattered floor. All but Stick's. He still hadn't made up his mind. Sounding a lot more confident than I felt, I taunted him.

"I hope you're going to try it, Stick," I cocked the Dragoon again. That was all it took. He dropped his knife and unbuckled his gunbelt.

Tormenters are usually bullies and bullies are usually cowards. And cowards almost never stand alone. It was over, and I was almighty glad. My poor head and brain were letting me know I'd had it. My legs were getting shaky.

I pointed my pistol at the youngest looking of the bandits. "You!" I ordered. "Pick up Stick's knife and cut Mick loose. Carefully!" When he was up and on his feet I asked, "How are you doin' Mick?" There was blood seeping from a dozen scratches and cuts but only a couple of them looked at all serious.

"I'm just fine," he answered, his upper body shiny with a mix of sweat and blood. "In fact, I feel like beatin' the hell outta somebody." He moved to face his burly torturer. "And I think you'll do just nicely."

The burly bully's face showed a moment of fear at facing Mick alone, then he lunged. Mick kicked him hard in the groin, doubling the bigger man over and making him cry out. Mick said, "I don't think fair play is called for here," then he hit him twice in the face.

In a backward swing of his right arm Mick brought the side of his fist whistling around striking Stick just below his ear, cracking his jawbone.

"I think that'll do for now" Mick said, then joined me at the bar where he began treating his wounds with a clean towel dipped in bar whiskey.

Again I waved my pistol at the man who had cut Mick loose. "Gather up the weapons and set them here on the bar, then rejoin your partners. You men," I ordered, "Very carefully grab a chair and sit up to the big poker table. Your hands on top where we can see 'em." A flash of pain made me blink in a second of blindness. I couldn't last much longer.

With their weapons piled on the bar I was now out of ideas, and almost out of strength. I didn't know what to do with our 'guests.' Sooner or later one of their gang would think to look inside the saloon and we'd be in the soup again.

Mick grabbed three bottles of whiskey and a handfull of shot glasses. With a wink at me he put them on the table in front of the men. "Drink up, boys. You're out of the action now. Enjoy it while you can." He returned to the bar and continued to tend his cuts.

The disarmed warriors swore, muttered and looked a bit puzzled. One of them asked, "Why you bein' so nice? We ain't done you no favors."

"Well, in a way you did," Mick answered. "You didn't help Stick, here, with his knife play. I'm happy about that. You coulda made it worse."

Satisfied with that the men fell to work on the whiskey. I began to see Mick's plan. Get enough rotgut into these bandits and they'd be in no shape to fight.

Mick stopped licking his wounds for a moment to looked at me. "You're not looking so hot, Muddy. You all right?" I could hardly keep my eyes open. I was squinting from the pain and I was beginning to feel very tired.

I heard myself say, "No, not really." I was starting to fade when we heard bumping noises from the cellar. I snapped up, wide awake. Mick took the big Dragoon from me and stepped back, ready.

The trapdoor at my feet flipped open and Hoss appeared in the hole. Dad was right behind him. I remember I smiled at him, then my lights went out again.

CHAPTER 17

I was back in Temporary Creek. This time there was a large whirlpool circling slowly. I could see it ahead of me as the thick black water carried me forward. I tried to get away. I tried to swim to the bank but the slow water was so thick that I could hardly lift my arms.

My legs could hardly move in the molasses-like fluid. I could hear Jonas's voice telling me not to give up. To keep trying. To keep my nose clean and keep trying. He was working on getting me out.

The current was pushing me and the whirlpool was pulling me in. Thick, dark water pushing and the whirlpool pulling. I tried to swim but I still couldn't move my arms or kick my legs. I was helpless. And Jonas was telling me to keep trying, that I could make it to the creek bank where Terp Finley was waiting to help me.

I tried to tell Jonas that Terp never helped me, that he always tricked me, but my voice wouldn't work. Then I saw a woman, her face hidden by her red hood, shove Terp into the creek. He was washed away.

The woman laughed, ran off a short distance then turned and threw back her hood. It was Dorrie! Her beautiful face was almost ugly. She laughed again and ran away.

Jonas threw me a rope. I felt better when I heard Jonas's voice. The water seemed thinner and my arms and legs could move better after I caught the rope. I could hear Jonas talking to Bill and Lud and Dad and Hoss, and the water became clearer and thinner and Dad was talking to me telling me that everything was all right. I walked out of the water.

I opened my eyes and saw Dad standing beside me. I was a minute getting my bearings. We were still in Mick's saloon. I was lying on one of his green-topped table. Dad was talking to Jonas. I thought I was still dreaming until Jonas spoke.

"I just got in this morning from Cheyenne. I understand you boys haven't exactly been staying out of trouble" Jonas grinned at his brothers and jokingly admonished them. "Is this what you two call keeping the lid on things?"

"Oh, it was all Muddy's fault." Lud said, grinning and pointing in my direction.

"Yeah," Bill added. "We were pretty much minding our own business when this kid started messin' with Judge Richardson and his good looking daughter." It made me feel good to hear my three "fathers" joshing each other the way they used to.

When Dad noticed that I was awake he moved toward the table. "How are you feeling, Muddy?

"I'm feeling pretty good, actually," I answered. "Guess that little rest was just what I needed." I noticed that it was daylight, that my head didn't hurt quite as much, and that the bandits were no longer sitting at their table..

"What happened to our guests," I asked?

"Hoss took care of them," Dad smilingly reported. "That man is one mean customer. He tied them to their chairs and set each of 'em in front of a window so their partners could see them, figuring they wouldn't shoot into the room. After a few minutes he pulled the blinds so they couldn't see us."

"Hoss did that?" I asked, surprised.

"Right," Dad went on. "Good plan, but it didn't work. The boys outside shot holes in two of their friends. The other three are half drunk and in jail. Took 'em across after daylight."

"So now what," I asked? "What's the plan for taking the judge out?"

Jonas spoke up. "I have all the evidence I need to put him in Laramie legally for a long time. Maybe for life. He'll never practice law again. Mavis Wertin and several witnesses are ready to testify. And I've uncovered a scheme of the judge's where he was giving some criminals shorter sentences in return for later favors. So let's pull in our horns a bit and you boys give me a chance to bring him in for trial."

It was Lud who reminded us of something. "Big brother, the first step in doing it your way is to have the proper authorities serve papers on the judge. Have you forgotten that we are those proper authorities and he flat out hates us? And right now his hired guns are waiting for us outside to cut us down the minute we show ourselves. Just how do you figure we're going to serve those papers?"

Jonas asked, "If they're outside waiting to shoot us why didn't they shoot me or try to stop me from getting in here a while ago when I first arrived?"

"I don't know for sure," Charlie said. "But it just occurred to me that all the people that the judge hates are cooped up inside here right now. All in one place! Maybe that's why they didn't stop you from gettin' in here. They could throw a couple o' sticks of dynamite in the window and blow us all to kingdom come. Think o' that, now."

Hoss interupted everyone's thoughts. "There's a rifle aimin' at us through the tall grass 'cross the street by the drugstore. Wasn't there a minute ago. Think mebbe they're gettin' ready to do somethin'."

Jonas said, "Anybody have a plan that would help us beat them to the punch?" That scared me. Jonas didn't have a plan. He always did. Now I was worried. But he wasn't quite done, yet. "Hoss, how many men does the judge have out there?

"Lemme see," Hoss mused. "He had ten, 'leven or so to start. Now there's four dead, an' three coolin' heels in the jail. That's seven. Prob'ly got five, maybe six more. Plus hisself and Dorrie. Could be eight or more in all. Whatcha got in mind?"

"Nothing, really," Jonas confessed. "Just that I like to know what I'm up against. Anybody else have any ideas?"

Bill suggested, "We could go out the cellar door and get around behind them."

"Yeah, but we don't know where they are" Lud argued. "Pretty hard to get behind them when we don't know where they are. Besides, there might be another rifle in the alley waiting for us to pop out of Mick's cellar.

"All right," Jonas said, taking charge. "Let's see about getting out of here. Hoss, you're the hawkeye in this group. Get into one of the front room windows upstairs and take care of that rifleman across the street. Roust him or shoot him. Your choice." Hoss happily agreed and headed upstairs.

"Muddy," he looked at me. "If your head is feeling up to it, you and Mick carry your Winchesters upstairs and take care of anybody hiding in the alley out back." To the others he said, "Bill, Lud, Charlie, and Jack. You boys and I are going to go out the front door as soon as they give us the 'all clear' from upstairs. Any questions.?"

"Well, I certainly have." It was my turn, now. "In the first place, now that I've finally have a father, I'm not figuring on losing him, and I hope he's not figuring on losing me. He's not going out there without me. No way! And in the second place, Charlie's got a wife and little girl in Wheatland. He has no business letting himself get killed over someone as worthless as the judge. I say Charlie covers the upstairs window; I go with you!" No one argued.

Dad was starting to protest when we heard a rifle shot from across the street and another from upstairs. Then we heard Hoss's voice yell down to us, "I called to him to put down his rifle and stand where I could see him. He thought diff'rnt. Now he don't think a'tall." He laughed at his own joke.

From the street we heard a call. It was Curly Wray. He was standing in front of the mercantile down the street. Close behind him were the judge, Dorrie and three men. Six in all. And all were well armed. The judge and Dorrie did not look happy.

"We got some talkin' t' do," Curly called. "Muddy, you get whoever's in charge of your people out here so's we can settle this."

Jonas was excited. "Now we're cooking! I'm always willing to talk rather than shoot." He looked at me. "Muddy, you know this man?"

"Yes," I answered. "He was my cellmate for a while. I'm not sure if I trust him, though." That did nothing to reassure anyone.

"You just gonna walk right out there," Dad asked? "We don't know how many of them there are, or where others might be hiding. I don't like this."

"Neither do I," Mick agreed.

"You're right," Jonas nodded. "Jack," he said to Dad, "I hope you don't mind a hard-nosed German borrowing one of your old Irish sayings about now: 'Trust everybody, but always cut the cards.'

"Charlie, Mick. Get upstairs and pick a window. Shoot anybody who isn't where he should be. Pass that word to Hoss. We're going out the front door as soon as we make sure our guns are loaded." This was the Jonas I knew. He had a plan and a way to go. This was the way I remember things being. I was seventeen, again.

CHAPTER 18

It was warm standing there in the street. The sun was a bit past eleven o'clock in the sky, not quite noon of a beautiful spring day. I heard another meadowlark, even here in the center of town.

A meadowlark is just about the most beautiful sound I know. It made the day seem almost perfect. Except for Curly and the judge and Dorrie and their bunch just a few hundred feet away, and all of us armed to the teeth and ready to shoot each other.

Death was just a short distance away and yet my mind chose to wander at such a time. The beautiful day, the song of the meadow lark, the quiet of the street. This wasn't real.

It surprised me to realize that I had been in Blainey for a week, almost eight days, and I had hardly laid eyes on Dorrie or the judge even though they were the reason for our being here.

Even from this distance I could see how beautiful she had become. No longer the pretty young girl. We closed the distance between us to about fifty feet. She was even more beautiful. We were looking at each other when I finally spoke. "Hello, Dorrie." Now, that was really brilliant! Six years ago I thought she was the most beautiful thing in the world. Now all I could say was Hello Dorrie.

"Hello, Muddy. Looks like prison was good for you." She was smiling but there was something wrong. It was her eyes. Her eyes didn't smile. They were hard and cold. What a shame. The rest of her was so beautiful.

Jonas did our talking. "Muddy says you're called Curly. No last name. You called this meeting so why don't you lead off. What's on your mind, Curly?"

"Well, we been talkin'. Us men. We hired our guns out for a range war. That's what we do." Curly explained. "But this ain't no range war. This is a vengeance fight. Not our kind o' thing."

At this the judge's head jerked up. Out in the bright light of day it was startling to see how he had changed. He had shrunk. His face was a hot red color and his nose was the terrible purple I had seen a few evenings ago in the lamp light of the Post House.

Curly said, "We're 'guns for hire,' all right, but we're still cowboys. We hire on and we ride for the brand. We'll help one rancher fight another over who owns what. When the smoke clears whoever wins gits paid. Whoever dies gits buried." The judge looked from Curly to the other men, eyes blazing.

"But I said we're cowboys. We don't fight the law. That gits a man put in jail. So we're backin' out o' this one. We want you to know so we don't get shot leavin'. What you do with them you already got in the jail is your choice."

Curly and the other three men, their pistols now in their holsters and their rifles cradled unthreateningly in their arms, began to back toward the side of the street where several horses were tied.

The judge screamed in fury, "No! You bastards hired on! You took the money! Now do your job, damn you!" He shook his shiny pistol at them.

Jonas called to him, "Odell Richardson, in the name of the law I order you to drop your weapon and submit to arrest."

"Arrest?" The enraged judge wheeled and fired at Jonas, missing him by a wide margin. While he was cocking his weapon to fire again the four lawmen reacted instantly, and returned deadly accurate fire. The judge was thrown backward into the dust of the street, his body jerking as each bullet struck. I hadn't moved.

Dorrie stood frozen, mouth agape, looking at her father's body, twisted by the impact of the bullets. It was all over, and I hadn't fired a shot. Then Dorrie turned back toward us. Without a word she raised her short-barrelled rifle and fired. The bullet thudded into Lud's chest. We were all stunned. Lud staggered backward, then fell.

Dad, Jonas and Bill stood frozen as Dorrie levered another bullet into the chamber of her rifle. In all their years as lawmen they had never shot a woman. They'd never had to.

I had no such feelings. Dorrie had just shot one of my "fathers." I drew and fired twice into her as fast as I could thumb my colt. But my aim, too, was somewhat hampered.

I could not bring myself to destroy her beautiful face. My first bullet struck her squarely in the chest, staggering her backward. Before she could fall my second bullet struck her inches from the first.

———◆———

We buried Lud King in the Blainey cemetery. I was pleased to see that most of the town, and people from several other communities, were at the funeral, testimony to the respect and affection the people of the area felt for these lawmen.

Also attending was Miss Mary Lynn Berg, who said she was resigning from her teaching position in Blainey. She had plans to return east to Madison, Wisconsin.

Two days later Roswell Denton buried his beautiful wife and her "Honorable" father in a double funeral that turned out to be the social event of the season.

It was attended by territorial governor Francis E. Warren and every district and county judge available, as well as many other officials of various importance. Their ladies accompanied wearing their wide-brimmed, floraled hats and long-sleeved gloves.

The judge was eulogized as a pioneer of law and order whose gavel had brought justice and jurisprudence to the wilderness of Wyoming Territory.

We'd been told to expect this kind of drivel so, as Miss Mary Lynn Berg might have put it, we were "not disposed" to attend for fear of nausea.

By now Charlie Gritt was back in Wheatland with his family. Mick Shane, after walking around bare-chested for most of a day to show off his scars, let Doc Feldt clean his wounds. He finally put on a clean shirt and got back to work behind his mahogany bar. Jonas and Bill King returned to Cheyenne and the law.

Jonas told us, "If we wait four or five months for things to settle down, I can begin 'helping' people learn about the judge's deals in sentencing the guilty. And Mavis Wertin still wants to testify. I think my friends on the parole board can be convinced that Ted, Pete and the Custis boys are not dangerous. With any luck at all, they should be out by this time next year. Maybe two years."

Dad and me made plans . . . I mean Dad and I. . .(blast you, Miss Mary Lynn Berg) planned to head northeast into Dakota Territory by way of Deadwood.

Hoss Hayes had a decision to make. Ross Denton and all his wranglers wanted him back in the Diamond D kitchen. However, Mrs. Ellie Finley wanted to keep him in her kitchen at the Post House Cafe. To help with the cooking, of course, so she said.

Hoss blushed, grinned and fidgetted whenever she looked at him. And she looked at him a lot as she touched her hair and smoothed her apron.

CHAPTER 19

The night before Dad and I were to head out for Deadwood Hoss came to our room upstairs over Mick's. "Would you boys mind if I trailed along with you? Maybe jist as far as Deadwood?" he asked. "I never seen Dakota an' I hear Deadwood is sumpthin."

After figiting a bit he came right out with it. "Miz Finley's a fine an' handsome woman, but I'm too old and into my own ways t' start learnin' about women an' such. Purely scares hell outta me"

"What about the Diamond D," I asked? "And that little boy of Ross Denton's?"

"Little Odie? Well sir, now," He smiled as he scratched his stubble. "I purely would like to be around to help young Ross raise that boy. Fact is, that child's gonna need some'un around who knows more than just whutch end of a horse takes the bridle."

He was looking at the floor, as he thought about this. "Sure would like to see Deadwood, though." Then he flashed a smile and changed the subject.

"What say we go down t' the Post House for a bite an' a cup? An' no need mentionin' to a certain lady what we been talkin' 'bout."

As we entered the cafe Ross Denton and Odie were just finishing their meal. When Odie saw Hoss he jumped down from his chair, shouted Hoss's name and ran to the rangy old man, laughing and pulling on his hand.

"Hoss," the boy smiled up at the old wrangler. "Can we have biscuits for breakfast tomorrow?"

Hoss smiled fondly at him, looked at Dad and me, let out a deep breath and said, in happy resignation, "Maybe I'll hafta see Deadwood 'nother time, boys." He let Odie pull him by the finger back to his dad's table. "You betcher life we can have biscuits fer breakfast."

Next morning it was just the two of us on the trail to Dakota Territory. A pair of Jacks heading for the poker tables at Deadwood. As we rode I began thinking of starting my sixty-third dreadful. I already had the title, "Who says a full house can't beat a Smith and Wesson?"

Willy T's
"Strike"

Cherry Creek's water level, in the eastern foothills of the Colorado Rockies, often rose and fell responding to the weather. If it rained the water level was high. If it didn't the creek was low. Simple water physics. Add to this the large rock – almost a boulder – that sat on the claim of a panner named Willy T and we have the makings of our story.

The rock was a nuisance. It was in Willy's way and Willy was plain damn tired of it. It had been either under water or totally exposed off and on for centuries. Just now it was high and dry. Willy decided to get rid of it by rolling it out of his way. Using a tree branch for a lever he managed to tip it over – and froze.

His heart pounding. his knees trembling, he was gaping at what every miner dreams of but so few ever see. A "glory hole!" A collection of nuggets and granules of nearly pure gold deposited a grain at a time by water crashing into the large rock and slowing enough to drop its lode onto the sand under and around the rock's depression. Hundreds of years of nature at work.

He almost shouted in his excited joy. Recovering, Willy looked around. No one was near. But someone always wanders by in a mining camp. He came alive. Quickly he gathered as many nuggets as he could, his fingers stumbling with excitement, and stuffed them into the pouch he kept inside his bulky coat. The pouch, always kept out of sight of the hunters, had a long thick cord that wrapped around his waist.

Every gold camp had it hunters, men who never worked a sluice box or panned the sands of the river bottom looking for their own gold. Instead they patroled the river banks of the camp watching for those who did, ready to take their strike from them – even if it meant killing them. Pirates.

Willy knew he needed a plan. He leaned on his branch lever a moment. He deliberately left several small nuggets – the size of wheat kernels and smaller – in the red sand and scattered more sand over these to hide them until he was ready for them to be "found."

Acting as casually as his pounding heart and trembling legs would allow, Willy ambled to the small fire in front of his tent. His plan was already forming in his mind, but he still needed to think. Slowly. Calmly.

He sat on the long, bleached log that earlier flood waters had left behind, and poured hot water from his coffee pot into his tin cup. His coffee supply had long since been used up. But that would soon change, he thought with inner excitement. Steady. No excitement.

If any of his panning friends would have noticed Willy just then they might have thought he was dazed or dreaming. He was staring blankly while his mind was racing forming the plan, steadying his pounding heart and trembling legs. After several minutes he was ready.

With a loud shout he threw the water from his cup and shouted, making sure that all nearby heard, "Dammit! Dammit all t' hell. I'm sick o' drinkin' hot water. I'm going to the settlement! An' I'm comin' back with some coffee."

Miners from several nearby claims looked up and smiled. Most had felt the same way at one time or another. One of them yelled back, "Go get it Willy. I'll be glad to help you drink it." Others laughed.

Willy borrowed a mule from a neighbor, after promising to share his coffee, and set out for the settlement. He made it a point to stop at several claims to show a pitifully small sack of dust and ask, "Do you think that's enough to get me a pound of coffee and a slab of bacon? I'm through drinkin' hot water."

In this way, Willy hoped he fooled the hunters. When he reached the settlement his first stop was the Wells Fargo bank. His nuggets were worth more than one hundred and eighty thousand dollars.

In a panic of excitement he wanted to leave from the settlement right now, take the stage to Denver and flee back to Dakota Territory. But the stage didn't go out until early the next morning. And the settlement had hunters, too. Watching. He forced himself to go back to his claim with the coffee and bacon and put the rest of his plan to work.

Back at his claim he pretended to find the small gold pieces he'd left in the sand. He shouted, "Nugget!" Then a few minutes later, "Nugget! And another one! Oh my God!" Everyone in the camp came running.

The 'lucky' panner showed them the nuggets and called for a cup to put them in. By the time he had found nine tiny nuggets the entire camp was around his small claim laughing and talking.

Someone shouted, "Let's weigh 'em, Willy." Willy got his pan balance. Another panner brought a set of weights. With the whole camp watching, Willy weighed his "strike."

An older veteran miner proclaimed, "Willy. You gotcherself close to two hundred, maybe even three hundred dollars there."

Willy shouted, "It ain't enough to take me back to Sara Jane in Pembina County, but the coffee an' beans an' whiskey are on me, boys." Cheers went up from the crowd. "Let's get some provisions down here from the settlement," he shouted. "I need to stretch an' holler."

Pembina County was in Dakota Territory where Willy had been working for Sara Jane's farmer father, who would not hear of his daughter marrying a mere hired man. With a promise to return rich, Willy set out for Colorado where they were picking gold out of streams . . .or so he'd been told.

There is very little in a mining camp to liven the gold mucker's day. It's filled with the hard work of digging, shoveling and panning, and going to bed tired and hungry and still broke. So when one of their neighbors runs into a little luck they drop their shovels and come help with the happy hell raising.

It took a while to get the celebration going, but once it started it continued through the evening and into the darkness of the night. It was after midnight – when even the hunters were sleeping soddenly and soundly – that Willy quietly left the Cherry Creek camp forever.

With his Wells Fargo certificate of deposit wrapped around his leg, between the two dirty socks he wore, he boarded the Denver stage in the settlement early the next morning. No one in the camps would ever see Willy T. again. He was in Pembina County, Dakoa Territory holding Sara Jane's hand.

Old Hoss

"**G**ood boy, Old Hoss. You're doin' fine. Just fine." I talk to my horse a lot. Man who's out in the 'by yourselfs' a lot gets a little hungry for the sound of a human voice, even if it's his own. So does his horse. We have a lot of one-sided conversations, Old Hoss and I do. Fact is, if I'm quiet too long he looks around to see if everything's all right.

I call all my animals 'Old' something. My last horse was Old Girl. Before her I had Old Boy. Now it's Old Hoss. We've been together maybe four years now. It's comforting to him to hear my voice so I talk a lot.

Bought him off a burnt-out lookin' fella in Pykeston. Fella couldn't have been more than thirty-five years old. Man's got no business being burnt out at that age unless he's had a whole life time of hard luck and failure. That fella surely had that beat down look in his eyes.

I gave him fifty dollars and got my bill of sale. He headed right into the Lonely Lady saloon. I felt a little guilty paying only that much for a horse I could see was worth a whole lot more, but I figured whatever I gave him would just be spent on a week's drunk. Appeared I figured right.

As I said, that was four years ago but the reason I remember it so well was what happened next. I turned to lead Old Hoss away and found myself facing two bare-foot, dirty-faced youngsters wearing mighty beat up clothes. A fine looking boy about ten and a girl about eight or so with blue sparkly eyes that took your breath.

"You just buy our horse, mister?" the boy asked.

That stopped me. All I could muster was, "Well, uh. . .well..."

"You'll like him," the girl said. Her eyes could have melted pigiron "His name's Charlie. Papa trained him to be gentle. Stands real still while I get up on him no matter how long it takes me. You'll take good care of him, wontcha?" They were not happy about this and I didn't like what I was beginning to feel.

I'm a traveling man, I tell myself. Just passing through on my way to see my sister two counties over. I got no time for this. I only stopped here 'cause my other horse – Old Girl – brought up lame and I needed a new animal. This isn't my town, these aren't my kids and this isn't any of my business. Besides, I didn't know the fella had kids. That's what I told myself.

"That fella your pa, is he?" They both nodded. "Live around here, do you?" They nodded again. "Where 'bouts?"

The boy got busy looking me over so he didn't answer, but the girl did. "Our place is about four miles straight out and then a half mile off the road."

The boy must have decided I was O.K. 'cause he joined in. "We got nearly five hundred acres of good grazin' land. Dad was raisin' registered breeding cattle 'til Mom got hooked by one of the steers last summer. . . . and died." His voice trailed off a bit.

"Here, son," I said. "You hold these reins for me; I'll be right back."

"He don't need to have his reins held," the girl said.

"Don't say 'he don't,'" I corrected her. "It's not lady-like, and you look like a fine young lady to me. Say 'he doesn't'"

When I'm the one talking I take every short cut in the world, even though I know well better. But it sounds bad and unschooled coming from a youngster's mouth. Especially such a pretty one.

Heading into Cooperman's general store I kept telling myself that this was none of my business and these were not my kids. But kids are everybody's business. Especially kids in that kind of shape.

"Mr. an' Missus Cooperman?" I asked the two folks behind the counter –I hoped that's who they were. "There's two youngsters out front in pretty sorry lookin' clothes. You bring 'em in here an' fit 'em' in clean duds from the skin out, from top to toe. Tell 'em their daddy gave you the money a while ago, or something. Whatever. I'll be back to settle for it directly."

They both looked at me as if they were going to say something, but I walked out and headed for the Lonely Lady.

Walking through the doors of that place I kept telling myself this is none of my business. I kept telling myself if that fella is a no good drunk that's just too bad. I'm sorry for those kids, but that's it. 'Course, I'm a total damn liar, but that's what I was telling myself.

Walking from bright sunlight into a dark saloon leaves a man blind for a minute or two. I couldn't see that fellow anywhere.

"Barkeep, there's a fella just come in here, but I don't see him. Is there a back door?"

"Whattaya want him for, mister?"

"Don't really want him a'tall, but he's got two youngsters outside who are kinda anxious about him. Where'd he get to?"

"You a lawman?"

"Me, a lawman?" I repeated. "Lord-n-then-some, that'd be the day. Nope. Fact is I'm nobody an' nuthin' this town's ever seen b'fore. I'm just passin' through on my way to Esterville t' see my sister. Bought this man's horse and . ."

"You bought Charlie?" He said it like I'd just spit on the church floor. "Well that about does it. Now they got no animals left at all."

"Friend," I slowed the conversation to a whoa and stood eye to eye with him. "I feel like I missed the whole first act of the school play. Would you mind fillin' me in here an' there so I know if we're talkin' about the same thing?"

He came back at me with, "S'pose you tell me your name and business, first."

"Fair enough," I stuck my hand out. "I'm Aldor Buckthorn. Used to hail from Cheyenne. I hail from a good many places now days, most of which I'm still welcome back to. Wrangled cattle most of my life. Your turn."

"Elder? You a church man?"

"Nope. It's AL-DOOR, an' I answer well to Al or Buck." I could have told him I was close to fifty, but I didn't. Could have told him that I was married once upon a time, but I didn't. And if I'd wanted to brag I could have told him that I'd earned my high school diploma, but I didn't. "How 'bout you?" I asked. "What do you answer to?"

He relaxed then, shook my hand with a grip that felt like he might have milked twenty cows a day at one time. "Louis Born," he said. "But my customers just yell out 'Lou'. S'pose you want t' know 'bout them kids. Elizabeth and Marcus Olsen – Betsy and Mark." I nodded.

In the next two minutes I learned that they were good kids, their mama was strong, their papa was weak. She died and he climbed into the bottle. He sold off his stock one drunk at a time. "Their horse Charlie was the last of it. Almost more a pet than a horse."

I said, "You tellin' me I should leave the horse with them? That it?"

Lou Born surprised me. "Nope. He'd just sell it to someone else and drink it up. Right now he's back in the corner with his bottle. Olsen's his name. He's my friend and I've tried to help him, but he just won't be helped. Way he's goin' he'll be dead in a year. We're good folks in this town, Buckthorn. We each got our own families to see to, but we'll see that those kids make out. You keep Charlie."

———◆———

Esterville was a hard day's ride from Pykeston if you pushed your animal, and a day an' a half ride if you went easy. Old Hoss an' I went easy, giving us time to get acquainted and ruminate a bit. Couldn't get those kids off my mind though, and that led me back to thinkin' of my wife, Ellie – Eleanor Mae Dokkus. Most everything leads my thinking back to Ellie.

She came to cook for the ten of us men on the Two-Star ranch – where I was head wrangler – a couple of years after her husband passed. She had soft eyes, a warm smile and gentle disposition. In a week every one of us was in love with her. 'Specially me.

After the sixth or seventh day of lookin' at her over the top of my coffee mug – she knew I was looking, too – I decided to make a social call at the dining hall while she was cleaning up after supper. Good thing I did.

A new hand – with the unlikely name of Joe Smith – was making a grab for Ellie. He looked mean and she looked scared. She had a big iron skillet in her hand but I could see it was too heavy for her to use well.

In a loud voice I said, "Well, now!" to make my presence known.

Smith spun to look at me and snarled, "I seen her first. You clear out of here. This ain't none o' your business."

While Smith was glaring at me Ellie grabbed that skillet with both hands and swung it at his head. She laid him out on the floor. Then she did what women do. She dropped the pan and started to sob. I did what men do. I wrapped my arms around her and let her cry.

I hope every man in the world has the chance to come running to the aid of a fair maiden, and gets to hold her in his arms while she cries. God, it's wonderful.

Almost every night after that we sat in the dining hall while the stove cooled. I smoked, she sewed and we visited.

One night she said, "Aldor. Do you have anything I could mend for you?"

I don't know what that means to folks in Chicago or Denver, but in cattle country that's just about a marriage proposal. A month later we got married and I never knew such happiness.

Our happiness lasted almost six years. Until she tried to give me a baby and died. And then I never knew such misery and loneliness. I just couldn't stay on at the Two-Star. That's when I became a traveling man. And it was about then I started thinking of looking for my little sister.

I hadn't seen Annie since she ran off with a handsome, no good, charming bottom dealer nearly twenty years ago – Mr. Royal Diamond by name. Now what kind of man has a name like that? I told her the man was no good, but she was young and in love. She slapped my face and stormed off. That was the last we saw of each other.

He took her to gambling halls in Colorado, Wyoming, Utah and Nevada while his luck was good. When the cards turned on him – actually, he got caught bottom dealing and the word got around – they finally settled in the town of Esterville, south east of Denver. It took me some time and a good bit of searching to find them.

Annie was hanging somebody else's wash on the line when I rode up to their run down little place on the edge of town. I called out from a short distance, "Halooo my pretty sister. It's your Bucky Boy!"

At the sound of my voice calling out my old nickname she let out a shriek, dropped the clothes she was hanging, and ran to meet me – arms out, skirts flying. Our hugging and kissing was enough to make neighbors talk.

I stepped back to look at her. My smile died. My sister's pretty face was lumps and scars from several years of beatings, and there was a recent bluish-red bruise near her eye.

"I'll kill that son-of-a-bitch," I fumed. "I'm gonna kill him!" I must have shouted it 'cause Annie hushed me.

After she got me calmed some she said, "He's not worth killing, Bucky. I won't have you going to jail for killing the likes of him. Let's just go away. I'd have left long ago but I had no place to go with the Mom and Dad gone. And I didn't know where you were. But now you're here. Let's just go."

While she was gathering her few things together Mr. Royal Double Dealing Diamond himself drove up in a one horse rig. When he saw me he turned to run but I grabbed his coat tail, pulled him out of the rig and spun him around. He had a two-shot Derringer in his hand – one of those gambler's hide-out specials – and fired too quickly.

The shot came close enough to ruin my hearing for an hour but missed me otherwise. I caught hold of his hand inside mine, forced the gun against his belly. Our struggling fired the second shot into his gut. Maybe I helped it just a bit.

I didn't want to kill him. I wanted to beat the living hell out of him. I wanted to pound him with my fists. Break his bones. I wanted to hear them snap. I hated this man. Instead here he was lying in a heap at my feet, blood running out of him. So now what?

I should have been happy. I should have said, *Serves you right, you damn woman beater.* I should have said, *Lie there and die, you son-of-a-bitch.* I should have said, *Bleed to death. See if I care.* That's what I should have said. What I wanted to say.

But I'm just not a man to kill things. I picked up that woman-beater and threw him back into the rig, got in and drove that horse hell-for-leather back up the street into town yelling, "I need a doctor." Somebody found one.

I said, "Doc, this man's got a bullet in him."

The doc said, "This man is dead."

Seems everybody in Esterville – especially the sheriff – knew Diamond for what he was and wondered how he'd escaped being shot this long. The sheriff just shook my hand and wished us well.

———◆———

I hadn't planned on being back in Pykeston so soon but Annie and I had no place we had to be so we were heading for Denver, and it was almost on the way. Besides, I wanted to check on those two Olsen kids. I left Annie sitting in the rig, with Old Hoss tied on behind, and went inside the Lonely Lady

This early in the day Lou Born was alone, sitting about where he'd been when I left him. We howdied and he told me, "You weren't gone an hour when Olsen got into an argument with one of his drinkin' friends. Got himself killed. No witnesses, so you might say 'the jury is still out' on that." He said it with a wry look.

"To make it worse, the drinkin' friend – he's got a name, but we just call him 'Boozer'– said he bought the ranch from Olsen just before the fight. Had a paper that said so. Jury's still out on that one, too." Another wry look.

"He's livin' on the place and keeps a loaded shotgun. The kids are scared of him and are hidin' out somewhere. We need to find 'em to prove the signature on that paper is forged. We're not gonna let him rob those kids."

'Course not, I thought. But so far it appears nobody's done anything. And it's been more than a week. So much for the good intentions of the good folks of Pykeston.

"Are you saying those two youngsters are alone and hidin' from a drunk who's livin' on their place and keeps a loaded shotgun. And nobody's out hunting for the kids? Thought you said this town was was gonna look after them. What kind of place is this, anyway?"

"Now cool down. Near everybody has been out, one time another, searching high and low. We've all tried. Search parties and such. No luck."

So what are you doing sittin' in town, I asked myself. Why aren't you still out looking 'til you find them. . . or their bodies?

I was steamin' mad. I untied Old Hoss and told Annie to find us some lodgings for the night 'cause I had business about four miles out of town. None of my business, of course, but I had to see for myself just how things were with those kids.

Now, I'm not exactly a field general, but I'm not a damn fool, either. I knew better than to ride right up to the front door of a man like that. I circled around to get the barn between me and the house and just rode Old Hoss right through the corral and up inside the back door of the barn.

I said I'm no damn fool. Don't put money down on that. The new "land lord" was crouching inside one of the stalls with both barrels of his long tom aimed at Old Hoss and me.

After looking me over pretty hard he said, "It don't appear you carry a weapon." The shotgun was holding on my belly.

"No sir," I said, holding my coat open to show him. "Never needed to. I get along well with most folks." All that was true. And I didn't carry a gun. But my horse did. I always kept a Walker Colt 'Dragoon' hanging in a saddle holster. For bears and cougars and such. The 'land lord' couldn't see it from where he stood.

You ever see a Walker Colt? Blame thing's a monster. It's close to a foot and a half long, weighs more than four pounds and fires a .44 caliber ball. It's a small cannon. Not a gunfighter's 'quick draw' weapon. It really is a horse pistol, meant to be carried in a saddle holster, with a Texas Ranger in the saddle.

Satisfied that I was no threat, Boozer eased his grip on the shotgun just a bit and was about to say something when the straw pile between us moved and the boy – Markus Olsen – poked his head up. The girl was beside him in the straw.

The barrel of the long tom bumped the side of the stall when Boozer spun around, otherwise the discharge would have killed the boy. In a second I was off my horse and crouched on my feet with the Dragoon pointed at Boozer chest.

"Now you just hold steady, mister," I cautioned Boozer.

Boozer was not a smart man. He screamed, "You lied! You did have a gun." He swung the shotgun back toward me. I had no choice but to pull the trigger.

The Dragoon sent a shock up my arm that was something awful, but it was nothing compared to what it did to Boozer. It lifted him off his feet and slammed him back against the wall, doing a pretty good job of killing him. Those two youngsters saw that. But they surely surprised me. It didn't faze them a bit.

I guess we expect kids to react to things the way we adults do. These two very young people had just lost their father, and the man who killed him was now trying to steal their home. They'd had just about enough time to work up a good hate for Boozer. Now he was dead. When you think about it, it's a wonder they didn't cheer out loud.

"Mr. Thorbuck," Standing next to her brother and holding on to his arm, little Miss Betsy was all smiles. "You brought Charlie back." Those two kids, wearing new but slightly dirty clothes, were more excited to see their horse than they were over the mess made by the Dragoon.

"Actually, kids," I said, "My name is Buckthorn. And I want you to come with me to meet my sister. She's waiting for us back in town."

With Betsy up on Charlie – we decided Old Hoss wasn't that much of a name after all – and Mark up on Boozer's nag, and with me walking between, we headed back into Pykeston where I had a visit with the town marshal, who was a man too old for the job.

When I asked why he didn't have a search party out looking for those kids he got a little red in the face, told me about his rheumatism and back problems, and sent some folks out to tend to the mess I'd left in the barn. He said he'd considered the matter closed if I would. I figured it was as close to an even trade as I was going to get.

Bad as things were, the morning's events didn't bother the youngsters' appetites in the least. It'd been over two days since they'd eaten. Those children ate a dinner that would have impressed a lumberjack. Then we spent a good part of the afternoon just sitting in the cafe getting better acquainted.

Lots of folks came around to shake our hands, Annie's and mine, and say howdy to the kids, but nobody offered to give them a place to stay, a home, or even take them in for the meantime. I began to wonder what kind of town and people I was seeing here.

After a while the kids began to get restless. Mark said, "Mr. Buckthorn sir, we'd like to go home, now. Betsy an' me'd like to sleep at home to night."

"'Betsy and I,'" I corrected, then added, "But son, there's no one out there. You're too young to be left out there all alone." There I was again. Getting my nose in where it didn't belong. I kept telling myself that this was none of my business. Then little Betsy spoke up. Her voice was like bells in my heart.

"Maybe you could let Charlie stay with us for a while." Her eyes had a real sparkle, and Annie had fixed her hair a bit. "And maybe Mrs. Diamond and you could stay with us just for a couple of days, since you don't have no kids to worry about."

"'Don't have any kids,'" I corrected. "Yes Honey, but we're travel...'

"Why I think that's a splendid idea," Annie chimed in. "I need to rest my back after the ride in that rig all the way from Esterville. Maybe we could stay just for a few days, Dear. What do you think, Bucky?"

"Well ... sure. For a couple of days, I guess."

As I said, that was four years ago. For four wonderful years my sister Annie and I have been helping raise two of the greatest young-sters in the whole wide world. They go to church; they go to school. They bring us their report cards. They even call us Uncle Buck and Aunt Annie. Kind of nice having a family.

Damn Town

I suppose I was a sight, a man my age slogging into the saloon like that. Winchester in my hand, saddle bags over my shoulder, chilled clear through and still wet. Nobody smiled or offered a word of welcome.

I laid my gear on the bar and walked over to the potbelly in the center of the room. Everybody seemed interested in me but nobody spoke so I opened the dance myself.

"Bartender I could sure use a double of rye to help this stove warm me up." I smiled nicely when I said it. Hell of a lot of good that did.

The barkeep didn't move. Instead he said, "Where you from mister, and what's your bi'ness here? You workin' for Cranberry? And while we're at it, where's your horse?" Cranberry?

A fella could just feel the friendliness pouring out of every dead face in that room. I took a breath, chewed on my lip a bit and told myself this was his town, not mine. Might be he had reason. It was clear enough no one else in the place was on the town's hospitality committee, either.

I didn't need a newspaper – if the town had one – to tell me there was something wrong around here. Got that feeling a couple blocks back just walkin' into it.

Maybe that was part of it. I was walking; carryin' my gear. Had to leave Old Girl standin' on three legs four or five miles back beside the creek where we fell in.

My fault. I didn't see the drop-off under the murky water. She screamed like all hell when we went down, me half under her in the mud.

Nearly cried when I saw how swollen her ankle was. That good animal'd been carryin' my butt and boots more than eight years. We were family. And I had to leave her alone out there while I looked for a vet. Either that or shoot her.

No sir! Not Old Girl. Not 'til I had a vet look at that leg, anyway. Then if it had to be done, I'd do it myself.

Thinkin' like that I was already sad and mad and soaked clear through when I hit that saloon. The mid-October breeze comin' off the Colorado foothills wasn't all that warm and friendly, either. Maybe that's what made me think I was not going to like this town. It looked all right – lanterns and candles starting to show in friendly looking windows – but I had an itchy feelin'.

I should tell you my name is Jackson Paul. I'm a blacksmith. I'm good at it, too. And strong. I'm nearer sixty than I am to fifty, but I've faced up to men lots younger and come away the winner. My hands are hellaciously strong. Been known to brag a bit now an' then, too, I guess.

I lived a gentle life up until Beth died ten years ago. A good wife, a good life, a good smithy in a good town. A good life. Up 'til then, anyway. No kids, so I just started wanderin'. Never lacked for work wherever I went. Small towns or big ranches, seems everybody needs a good blacksmith. As I said, I'm one o' the best.

Blacksmith or not, I still got good manners and know how to read. Mother was a school teacher b'fore she married Dad. She liked Shakespeare, so I do, too. She liked to cook, so I do, too. Mother didn't like being called Ma so I called her Mother. Show me a boy who doesn't like what his mother likes.

Dad was a fine blacksmith. He taught me everything. I couldn't call him Pa 'cause I couldn't call Mother Ma. And he really liked being called Dad, so no 'Ma and Pa' in our house.

I can read an' write an' shoe a horse, recite a little Shakespeare and make a fine apple pie. How many blacksmiths do you know who can do all that? My folks figured I'd make out all right in the world.

Anyway, walkin' into town I looked for the nearest saloon. Great places for strangers, saloons. There's food, friendliness, usually a warm stove and lots of local information. Maybe even a veterinarian. Usually.

"Gentlemen," I addressed the room. "As soon as I get my two fingers of rye I'll trade you answer for answer. I have questions, too." The barkeep thought a moment longer, then brought me my drink.

"What's this about Cranberry?" I asked anyone.

A big kid of about twenty-five or so swaggered up in front of me. I'm not a small man but if I'd stood close up to him you could have seen him showin' above and on all sides of me, and I'm about six feet. He was big.

"Mister, you must think pretty much o' yourself waltzin' in here like you own the place. We'll ask the questions and you'll answer them." As he spoke he reached for my shirt front to make sure I understood. I don't like young men who strut and talk tough to older men.

I've seen his type in lots of places. Some of them are just big kids stretching their wings. But some are bullies. Big blow-hards who lord it over kids, little women, old men and three-legged dogs. Seldom tackle anyone their own size. It's a type I don't like. Got no use for them.

I caught his hand before he got to my shirt. Years ago I learned a cute trick that a smaller man can do if he can get hold of the little finger of the bigger man, before the bigger man gets set, and squeeze it just right. No great effort to it. I did that. The big kid let out a terrible yowl of pain and dropped to one knee ka-plop, agony on his face. All he could say was "Ow! Ow-ow!"

After a few seconds I eased the pressure on his finger, but didn't let go. I said, "When you get up are we gonna fight or be friends?" He got his hand back and stepped away from me, uncertain what to do next. Before he had time to decide the bartender spoke up.

"Hold on now, Thermon. He didn't break your arm or kill you, an' you did sorta ask for it.. Let's leave well enough as is 'til we see what we know here." To me he said, "O.K. mister. Your turn. Who are you and what 'r' you doin' here in Gault?"

"Thank you. Well, I'm a wandering blacksmith," I began. "Used to live in. . .."

"Blacksmith?" A plaid-mackinawed man about my age sitting near the stove sat up straighter. He was the first person to offer a smile. "Mister, good or bad don't matter. If you be a blacksmith you got yourself a home right here. Uh ... if you like. We got us a first rate blacksmith shop but no blacksmith." A few heads nodded. A few faces even smiled.

The bartender – Jeeter, it turned out – volunteered, "We had a good one but he had the bad habit of pattin' our women here an' there. A committee of us husbands took up the bi'ness of helpin' him relocate."

"Jeeter," the mackinaw said. "You're leavin' out the best part. We took him out past the creek, took his pants an' boots, then ever so sweetly directed him to get the hell out the county an' don't never come back." Everybody in the place had to smile on that. A few laughed, remembering. So did I, but I was getting anxious about Old Girl.

Jeeter added, "Answerin' your question about Cranberry – Canterbury, actually – owns most of the land around here plus the mercantile, the hardware and grain an' feed stores. Figures his vote's worth five of anybody else's. Tried runnin' for mayor and got shut out bad. He's been sore as a man with a boil on his butt ever since. Got his foot on the town's throat though, an' keepin' it there."

"Gentlemen, I'm sorry to show my impoliteness, but I had to leave my horse four or five miles back. Left saddle and tools, too. She got hurt when we fell into the creek. She'll be wonderin' if I've left her to the wolves."

No western man can turn his back on an animal in pain, especially not a horse. Especially not a good horse.

"I'd like to see to her needs first and answer your questions later, if you don't mind. Right now can you help me find a vet.?"

The man in plaid said, "No vet'inarian mister, but Mrs. John at the livery stable can do for you. She's a fair midwife, too." I didn't smile this time but I sure wanted to. A midwife. Just what I needed.

Making the ride back from Gault out to the creek, sittin' up along side Mrs. John – a mighty handsome woman, by the way – on the bench of that flat-bed wagon, I learned a few more things than I really wanted to know.

For instance: she was a widow and was I married, she asked? She smiled real wide when I said I was a widower. How long had I been running loose, she asked? What plans did I have, she asked? Any plans to settle in Gault, she asked? And where was I planning to spend the night, she asked? And did I know she had a room for rent, she asked? And did I know her name was Jennie – Jennie Cook?

I'm a healthy strong-made man able to care for myself and my own needs, but that woman had me more nervous than I'd been in some time. I was almighty glad when we reached the creek. Old Girl's head was up and her ears forward. She was always glad to see me. Now there was one female I understood.

Got to give Mrs. John – Jennie – her due, though. She knew what she was doing bringing this heavy flat-bed and all that harness. She pulled up close along side of Old Girl where the animal stood on her three good limbs.

She checked Old Girl's leg, proclaimed it a bad sprain, and started throwing the harness over her. "You ever see a tripping harness before?" she asked.

"Yes Ma'am, I surely have," I told her. "Had occasion to use one a time or two when tryin' to shoe a few mustangs."

A tripping harness is the dangdest thing you ever saw. Whole bunch of straps and buckles that you wrap around an animal, and when you pull the straps through the buckles just right that animal has no choice but to hunch down more and more 'til it has to lie down. In this case, right onto the flat-bed wagon. We were on our way back to town in no time, horse, saddle, tools and all. And Mrs. John started right in again.

"I suppose you're wondering how a woman comes to be running a livery."

"It crossed my mind," I tried to sound casual. Actually I was curious as hell.

"Beats starvin'," she said. "John – my husband – decided to die on me and left me with a mortgage on the house and stable, way too many bills and a boy to raise. The bank was real glad when I decided to stay and pay off the bills. Not that I had lots of choices. I was broke, had no place to go, and my boy Thermon was maybe fifteen at that time."

"Thermon? Your boy's name is Thermon? Big kid? About twenty-five or so?"

"Yep. He's the one you put to the floor in Jeeter's saloon this afternoon. He's a good boy but he has trouble minding his own business sometimes. It got him fired from Owen Canterbury's O-C ranch where he was keeping books and helping manage. Practically ran the place for him, really. By-the-by, that was a neat trick you used on his finger. You'll have to show it to me."

"You know about that, too, do you?"

"Yep. Know you're a blacksmith, too. And you drink rye whiskey. Don't have any in the house just now. I'll have to get some. You going to take that room or not? Our house is next door to the livery. Close to your horse."

—◆—

In the morning I went next door to check on Old Girl and get the blanket roll I had my metal working tools in. 'Girl' was fine, but didn't want to put any weight on the bad ankle. She nuzzled my arm and nickered, glad to see me. Now there's a good female or you.

I had told the men in Jeeter's that I'd be around for a few days while Old Girl mended and that I would set up in the town's smithy if they needed any iron work done. Figured I'd better get some breakfast into me and get a fire going in the forge before any of 'em showed up.

A block up the street I smelled bacon. It was a small town cafe with a big city name on the sign – *The Waldorf*. The door was open and the coffee and potatoes smelled good. Nobody needed to invite me.

This early in the day there were only a few customers. Three drovers at the first table were finishing their breakfast. At the second a frowning, well dressed man of about fifty was lingering over his coffee. I scuffed my feet as loudly as I could so they'd hear me in the kitchen, then took a chair at the only other table.

A friendly looking lad of fifteen or so came out to take my order. "You aren't the prettiest waitress I've ever seen," I kidded. "So you must be good." He saw the humor and grinned so I asked, "What's on the menu this morning?"

"Pretty much the usual, sir. Pancakes, bacon, sausage, eggs, your choice of biscuits or toast. Oh yeah. Fried potatoes and coffee, of course. And honey for the biscuits. You the blacksmith?"

My supper had been the two fingers of rye in Jeeter's saloon. I was ready to tackle a wild boar. "Biscuits? Really? I'll have one of everything except the biscuits. I want two of them. Yep, I'm the blacksmith. A hungry blacksmith. Can we start with that coffee right away?"

He grinned again. "Sure thing. Comin' right up. By the way, my name's Chad. Chad West. Me an' Mom own this place an' she's the best cook in the world."

I knew I should have left well enough alone and just let him get my coffee, but I had to put my foot in it. I had to ask. I had a feeling about this town.

"What does your dad do, Chad?" I had a notion what the answer was going to be so why the hell had I bothered to ask?

"Oh, Dad died a couple years ago. It's just me an' Mom now." This he said over his shoulder as he headed through the doorway into the kitchen. For just a quick second I felt a shiver. Like yesterday sitting up on that flat bed wagon next to Jennie - Mrs. John - Cook.

It took two plates to handle all the food the pretty, fortyish-looking woman carried from the kitchen to my table. "Good morning,

Blacksmith. This ought to hold you 'til noon. I'm Marion West, Chad's mother. Understand you spent the night at Jennie Cook's." Talk about getting right to it. "There are lots better places, you know". She touched a fixing hand to her hair and I lost some of my appetite.

"Pleased to meet you, Mz West," I politely came half way to my feet, then plopped back onto my chair. "You set a fine table, ma'am." I know what knife and fork are for so I set to work on the potatoes thinking this might discourage further conversation. No such luck.

"You planning on staying in Gault?"she asked. "We can always use a good man in the area. You planning on staying at Jennie's again? Where you plan on taking your meals? Chad and I could take good care of you here." She touched her hair again. This was turning into a not-so-good breakfast.

The fellow at the next table – the guy in the suit – came over. "I need to talk to you, mister." I was glad for the interruption, but he still hadn't smiled.

Marion West spun away and returned to her kitchen without speaking to the man, and I returned to my cooling breakfast, which really was one of the best I'd had in a long time. I realized I hadn't spoken to the man in the suit, either.

"Finish your breakfast, blacksmith, then join my men." He pointed to the three at the first table. "You can ride out to my ranch with them. I have several horses that need shoeing, and some wagon work. My name is Owen Canterbury." I'm glad he didn't offer his hand to me. I'm not sure I'd have taken it.

Dismissing me and any thought that I might possibly have an objection or an opinion, he started for the door. I said, "You must be the one folks in Jeeter's place called 'The Cranberry.'" A sudden flush of color in his neck told me he didn't like that name, which pleased me for some reason.

"Thanks for the invitation," I continued. "But I already told some folks I'd be on duty at the smithy shop this morning, first thing. Don't like to disappoint nice people so that's what I'll do. Soon as I finish there I'll come right on out to your place." More color in his face.

Before he left the cafe a very sober, serious, unfriendly and red-faced Mr Owen 'Cranberry' told his men, "See that he's with you when you ride out," and stomped out the door The men glanced my way. They did not seem pleased with their boss's order.

After a bit I paid my bill and stepped over to their table. "Gentlemen, why don't you walk with me to the blacksmith shop – you can even show me where it is – and we can discuss our next move."

The two younger cowboys, both in their late teens or early twenties, were not sure what to do about me. The other man – his face showed several seasons of riding into the wind – laughed and said, "Boys, let's walk with the man."

Considering that the town had no blacksmith, the shop was mighty well set up A good forge, working bellows, several hammers and mallets, some ferriering tools, several kegs of shoeing nails and plenty of nuts and bolts. I could fall in love with a place like this. Even lots of coal. Everything was covered with the dust of disuse, but most everything a shop should have was there.

I asked one of the younger men, "Would you lend me a hand and heft one of these kegs up onto that shelf for me?" Without hesitating he bent to the task and found he couldn't do it. A keg of horseshoe nails weighs eighty pounds or more.

"How about you?" I asked the other young drover.

"Do it yourself. We don't work for you," he responded. Well he was right about that, but he could have been a little less arrogant.

Laugh lines appeared again near the eyes of the wind-burned cowboy. "I think he just wants to see if you can do it, Jonesie."

"Hah!" Jones snorted. He grabbed the keg around the middle and raised it several inches off the ground before he had to let it slip back to the dirt floor.

There's always an easier way to do a thing. I tipped the nail keg forward enough to get one hand under the bottom lip. With the other hand on the top lip I took a step forward and swung the keg upward using the weight of my body instead of just my arms. I impressed them.

Facing the two younger men I said, "Gentlemen, I'm twice your age but I'm bull strong, and I know a lot of dirty tricks. If we have to fight you'll likely lose. And pick up some bruises in the process. I would, too, of course. I'm not going to the ranch with you today, and that's that. Now I have to get a fire started. Tell 'Cranberry' whatever you like."

The older drover did laugh this time and extended his hand. "Name's Jim Small, Blacksmith. I'll tell him. He'll likely fire me, but that's fine. Been gettin' ready to tell him what he can do with his ranch, anyway. Who knows, maybe I'll come back askin' you for a job." He laughed again.

I smiled back and took the offered hand, "Jackson Paul," I said. "Call me Jack or Paul. I answer well to either, 'specially 'round meal time." The three men left and I busied myself for the next hour with fire and forge and laying out my tools.

I'd been traveling a week or more when Old Girl and I took our dump in the creek. I hadn't had a heavy hammer or mallet in my hands in all that time. It felt good to pick up the five-pounder and stretch myself by swinging it over and around my head a few times.

"Well, aren't you the cute one." Her voice came from behind me. I almost dropped the sledge on my foot. "You always dance with a hammer? More fun with a woman." She grinned at me.

She was standing in the open double doors of the shop holding the reins of a team that was hitched to the buckboard behind her. Another team was tied to the back of the buckboard. She had happy eyes and a great smile. A little on the plump side, but happy eyes and a great smile. A bit of grey showing in her black hair.

Two youngsters – a boy and a girl maybe twelve years old – stood in the wagon box back of the seat. Twins, most likely. They looked like her except for their blond hair. The boy needed to have his nose wiped. Why is it always the boys who need this?

"Sometimes it's safer dancing with a hammer," I answered. "Can I help you?"

"So you're the blacksmith. I'm Brydee Nord and these are my twins, Erik and Athlone. Their daddy – big Erik – has been dead and gone three years now. I have three quarter-sections of prime land in the valley three miles out." She hardly paused for a breath.

"My teams need shoeing and trimming, and I'd be obliged if you could get to them right away. I still have corn standing in the field." Her happy eyes got serious for a moment. "Are you sleeping at Jenny Cook's again tonight?"

Wouldn't you think I'd be getting used to these questions by now? Not by a damn sight. "Yes, I'm the blacksmith. Yes I can see from here that your teams surely are in bad need of hoof work. No I haven't decided yet where to sleep tonight. And would you like to suggest where I might eat my supper this evening?" I put a little sarcasm into that.

"Maybe I am being a bit forward," she blushed. "But living out in the valley like I do gives Jennie Cook and Marion West the advantage with any new man that comes to town. Got to make my hay while the sun is shining, y' know."

"Let me get right to your animals," I told her. "so you can be on your way." Why didn't they name this town Widowville. At least Widow's Walk. Maybe even Mantrap. Then a man'd know enough to pass the place by. I knew there was something wrong with the town when I walked into it.

"No hurry," she said. "My youngsters will enjoy playing in the street with the town kids. I'll just sit here and watch you work. Nice to watch a man work." I had a little trouble picking up my shoeing tongs. All of a sudden too many thumbs on each hand.

I was beginning to figure this was going to be just one hell of a day in one hell of a town when cowboy Jim Small returned. "Mornin' Brydee." Her happy eyes lit up that whole part of the shop when she saw him.

To me he said, "I saw Owen Canterbury in front of Jennie Cook's stable just now. He re-hired her boy Thermon t' come back and 'keep score' at his ranch. I told him you weren't comin' out and that I wasn't going to push you. He fired me, just like I said he would." He was smiling. Brydee hadn't taken her happy eyes off the big cowboy since he walked in.

"Well, you don't seem too broken up about it," I said.

"I guess not." The smile widened. "Needed to get out of there. Talk about bein' in a rut. No plans where to go, p'ticlarly. Just feels good to be out of there. Mind if I lend a hand around here a while? I'm pretty good with a hammer and forge."

"You're a blacksmith?" That surprised me. "How come nobody around here seems to know it?"

"Nobody asked me, I guess. I'm a fair shot with a pistol, too, but nobody's asked me to be sheriff, either." He was smiling again. So was Brydee. "Bein' farm-raised I know a thing or two about farmin', too – corn an' pigs an' such."

I said, "Seems to me you'd be a number one bachelor on some-body's list." He reddened a bit and glanced at Brydee who was blush-ing radiantly.

Jim stammered, "How'd be if I clipped and filed the hooves on Brydee's animals while you're bendin' the shoes for them?"

Before I could voice my approval Brydee gushed, "Oh yes, Jimmy. That would be wonderful." Jimmy? Evidently these two go back a ways.

Shortly after lunch Chad West showed up. "Mr Canterbury and Mrs. John are sitting in our cafe having coffee an' cake, talking soft and smiling at each other. Mom told me to go find something to do for an hour. I think she wants to listen in. Mind if I hang around here a while?"

Brydee jumped up. "Jenny Cook and Owen Canterbury? In your mom's cafe. I wanna listen in, too. It's coffee time for me boys. Be back for my horses later." She didn't run. That wouldn't have been lady-like. But I don't recall ever having seen a woman walk any faster.

It turned out to be a pretty productive day after all. I got a lot of iron work done for folks, Jim got Brydee's four animals trimmed and shod, and agreed to help get her corn crop in – I'm betting they'll be engaged by the time the corn is in the crib – and Owen Canterbury and Mrs. John spent most of the afternoon sitting on a bench in front of her livery stable laughing and gigling like a pair of high school kids. Makes a fellow look forward to tomorrow.

———◆———

Three days later I was holding a hot horseshoe in my tongs when Jim Small showed up again. "I've been helping Brydee get the corn crop in. Not quite done yet, but I figured I'd better get in here and help you out some." He looked over his shoulder as if something – or someone – was chasing him.

"Oh, I can manage," I said, stifling a smile. "There's plenty enough work here, that's for sure. But I can manage. For a while, anyway.

This town surely does need a blacksmith. How are things coming with you and Brydee?"

You could tell I dropped my hammer on the right toe with that question. He folded right up, plopped down on a nail keg and proceeded to look almost sick.

"I used to dance and hug with Brydee Mohagen long before she married that big Swede," he was almost whining. "And it's nice doin' it again, now, each evening after her kids are tucked in. But in the daylight she's a full-time boss, orderin' me to do this, do that. Stack it here, stack it there. I had to get some air. So here I am."

I pretended to concentrate really hard on hammering that hot horseshoe into a curve around the small end of the anvil. "Are you asking me a question in all of this, or are you just letting off steam?"

"I guess I was wonderin' if that's what it's like bein' married?" He was already thinking marriage?

Every once in a while I say something that's really smart or make up a tall tale that's really good. I had a feeling I was about to do it again.

"Jim, when my Beth and I were first married she had me jumpin' through all kinds of hoops and givin' me all kinds of orders. One evening I put my arms around her, hugged her good, kissed her hard and said, 'Sweetheart anything you want you just ask. Just ask!' She got my point and we had a wonderful life."

The big cowboy got up off that nail keg smiling. He did about an hour's work and said, "I think I'd better head on back to the farm.. Got to get the rest of that corn in, but I'll be able to work maybe three days a week here in the shop." He went through the door still smiling.

I decided that my supper that night at the Waldorf Cafe would be my last. I was getting out. By the time I got the forge fire banked for morning, washed the grit off my hands and closed the shop doors most of Marion West's customers had eaten and left so she sat with me. Her part of the conversation got right to the point. Again.

"When are you going to move out of Jennie Cook's place and move in here with me so we can get married?"

Married? As I said earlier, you'd think I'd be used to the directness of the women in this town by now. Well, I wasn't. When I didn't reply she went right on.

"Well, Jennie's pretty well got her cap set for Owen Canterbury, and Brydee Nord seems to be well in command of that good looking cowboy. That leaves you and me as the single members of the town. How about it? Are you going to marry me or not?"

Diplomatically, weakly and cowardly I said I could not, would not and wasn't about to marry anyone just now. Most of this speech was courageously delivered as I backed toward and through the cafe door.

I skipped breakfast next morning and was hard at work when Chad West rushed in. "Mr. Paul! Mr. Paul! Come help! Right away, please. Mom's lying on the floor of the cafe. She can't get up and she can't talk. I couldn't find Mrs. John, and there's nobody else around. Can you help."

By the time we got to the cafe there was a crowd inside. Jennie Cook was already down beside Marion West, Owen Canterbury crouching next to her. In a quiet voice almost no one had ever heard Canterbury use before he said, "Jennie, I've seen this kind of thing before. She's had a stroke. I'd say it's a bad one."

To Chad he said, "Stay close to your mother, son." To Chad's mother he said, "Marion, I think you can hear me. If you have anything you want to try to say to Chad say it now." He stood up and addressed the crowd, "Folks! Everybody outside, please. Now, please. Out. Out, please." Owen Canterbury was certainly a man of surprises.

<hr />

Chad West's mother died that afternoon where she lay on the floor of the Waldorf Cafe. She was buried two days later next to her husband. Chad spent most of those two days with me in the blacksmith shop pretending to help me bend horseshoes.

For two days the people of Gault were without a coffee and social center. Chad finally realized that horseshoes were not his line. He re-opened the cafe and half the women in Gault tried to hire on as cooks and bakers. The Waldorf Cafe would surely rise again.

I figured it was time for me to hit the trail again – maybe Denver. Jim Small said he could spend three days a week smithing now that Brydee's corn crop was in. But Old Girl's sprain turned out to be a cracked bone. She'd never carry a rider again. I needed a horse.

Thermon Cook knew of a breeder in Kiowa County known to have good riding stock. He also had a forty-five year old, never-married daughter who lived with him. Or maybe he lived with her. Alarm bells rang in my head. So why didn't I just turn around and head the other way?

Some men can't stay away from the gambling halls. Others have a mean thirst for John Barleycorn. As for me, I'm just fiercely nosey-damn-curious. Not a gossip or a meddler, y' understand. But I've just got to see what's around the next corner, over the next hill, behind the closed door or in the next chapter of the Saturday Evening Post serial.

It was a two day trip in my rented rig, and all the way I kept asking myself why she lived with her Daddy. Prob'ly 'cause she's wart-hog ugly with a sore-tooth grizzly bear attitude and a personality like a November day. Then I met her.

She looked like sunshine and flowers, with a voice like soft summer rain. Her happy eyes were blue, with a personality that would brighten any day. The book under her arm was Shakespeare's "Much Ado About Nothing."

Turned out she never married 'cause she'd had to take care of her invalid father for all these years. He'd cashed in his chips just a month ago and she was selling off the stock.

I didn't know whether to turn and run or stay for supper. So I bought a good horse and sat down to talk a little Shakespeare with a very lovely lady.

~ Paying Back The Swede ~

"Hymie!," I almost shouted as I came hot footin' it into his office at the back of his store. "The Swede needs help! Blackie O'Rourke's holdin' a paper on his homestead an' it's due t'day." I was sweatin' a bit and lookin' over my shoulder. If Blackie knew I was trying to help our big friend, Hymie's and mine, there's no tellin' what he'd do about it.

Thomas "Blackie" O'Rourke wasn't all bad. Just mostly. And sometimes it made me a little embarrassed that he was Irish. Still, if the Monsignor asked him for it, he'd build him a new church. And mostly out of his own pocket. But where there's a dollar to be picked up, never mind whose wallet it fell out of, or might still be in, Blackie gets real aggressive.

It was my own mother, God rest her, who said it. "Scum rises to the top". And Blackie certainly had done that. And besides, there wasn't a Monsignor within 300 hundred miles of Grand Forks.

So I'm tellin' Hymie, "He needs $230 for the payment. He ain't got it, an' Blackie knows it. Blackie wants that hundred and sixty acres the Swede's filed on, an' he wants it bad. Right along the rail-road right o' way, y' know." I was a bit out of breath, myself. "He's sent four o' his dark-suited arm twisters out to Ojata to foreclose on him, so we ain't got much time. It's only eight miles."

Hymie's reaction was immediate. He jumped out of that squeaky tilt chair of his, stood his full five feet and four, ready to fight for our giant Scandinavian friend.

Several years earlier, in the spring of '82, Mike Ryan and I had shared a boxcar with the huge Norwegian immigrant – Gundarharl Lunde – and his family, along with their property and livestock. Many a pioneer traveler before us had arrived in this good land of opportunity in much the same manner.

Mike an' me could o' ridden inside on the cushions like reg'lar passengers, and for free being employees of the St.Paul, Minneapolis & Manitoba Railroad, but after helping this nice family load their goods and their animals we found them to be good company and thought we'd ride a ways, maybe as far as St. Cloud, in the boxcar with them, cow dung an' all.

We were watching a beautiful prairie sunset that evening, out of the open door of the boxcar. The train had just started to creep north out of the St.P.M.& M. railyard just before the point where the rails cut northwest on the Elk River-St. Cloud line headin' for Fargo, when we heard shouting and commotion along side the track just behind our car.

Several rough looking men, at least two of them with clubs, were chasing and swearing at a smaller man who appeared to be running for his life. As they came abreast of the door of our boxcar the Swede knelt down, grabbed the smaller, terrified man under the arm and lifted him onto the floor of the car with no more effort than if the man were a child.

Two of the pursuers managed to climb into the boxcar where the man with the club met a mighty Nordic fist that sent him very quickly back the way he had come. The second man had the good sense to jump before Gundar could reach him. The other pursuers immediately gave up the chase.

"Thank . . . you," our new guest panted. "you . . . saved . . . my life." He puffed, lying on the floor while his breathing slowed and his color improved.

"Vhy dey chase you," Gundar asked "Vot you do to dem?"

"N. . .nothing," he puffed. "Didn't . . . do anything. I'm . . . a Jew." He looked at each of us, then said, "Do I . . . stay . . . or go?" He was getting his wind back and his color was even better.

"Ye stay," I said, stepping forward, my hand extended. Mike and I had seen this sort of thing before back in Ireland, but big Gundarharl Lunde, youngest son of a farm family that hadn't enough farm for all the sons, had never known bigotry in his native Norway. The amazement of it showed on his face.

"I'm Willum Duffy," I continued. "That grinnin' mug over there belongs to one Michael Ryan, late of County Roscommon, as am I. And this big Swede who saved your bacon is Gundarharl Lunde. Back there's Gundar's wife Dorcas, and those two little cotton-tops are Nils and Eva."

"I don't be Svede" Gundarharl snorted at me, with just a little venom. "I be Nor-vid-jun!" Although none of us in that boxcar ever again called him "Swede" to his face, we would never call him anything else whenever we spoke of him behind his back. Gunderharl was just too big a mouthful. Especially after having lifted one or two at Shannahan's.

"I am Haim Mendl," the smaller man said, grasping the huge hand Swede offered, pulling himself to his feet.. "I am ... or rather, I was ... cook, waiter, bookkeeper and, sometimes cashier at the Rail's Head Tavern, near the 'yards'."

That was how we all met a good half-dozen years ago. All of us bound for Grand Forks, Dakota Territory and new lives. I was to become the new superintendent of track maintenance on the Larimore and Grafton lines, and Mike was to be the new section foreman. The head "gandy."

Swede and his family were bound for their homestead at Ojata just eight or ten miles further west. Hymie was "between fortunes," as they say. By the time the train reached "The Forks" we were well acquainted and good friends.

It wasn't long after our arrival before Hymie had a small but fast growing dry goods store half a block south of the tracks on Third Street. If you asked him for credit he would stand in front of you, hands grasping his coat lapels, sizing you up for half a minute. You'd best not blink.

If he liked your looks he shook your hand and you got your goods. He might even lend you cash money. If you fidgeted too much, or if your eyes kept looking away, Hymie's hands stayed on his lapels and you didn't get any credit. He seldom judged wrong.

It was rumored around town that he had his hand in a few other local enterprises as the silent partner of a few "good Christian people."

As I stood in Hymie's office this day the small man was all concern and business. "How do we get the money to him, Will?" he asked me, already reaching into his pocket for the key to the locked drawer of his desk where a scant few of us knew he kept his ready cash.

I told him, "Ryan and three good men are down at the tracks with a hand pumper. The Indian will take it to him. He's waitin' for me at your back door right now. Blackie's men are in a shay and they'll have to follow the curves in the road," I said.

"The rails run straight as a string the whole several miles. If Mike and the lads get goin' right away, they'll beat Blackie's boys to Ojata by a good half hour. And the Swede's homestead is just a stone's throw further. He'll be able to hand the money to the black suits the minute they step out of that buggy," says I.

Hymie counted out two hundred dollars in fifties and three ten dollar bills, then added twenty more in fives. "The Swede might need the extra," he said. "Tell Mike to tell the Swede he owes me just the two hundred thirty." He slapped the money into my hand and I ran the few steps to the back door where Joe Walks-The-Wind was waiting.

"Give this to Mike," I said. "And tell him to tell the Swede he's t' pay back all but twenty dollars. Tell him he's to buy somethin' nice for Dorcas out of the twenty. Now run!"

Walks-The-Wind was too much name for most of us to bother with, and there were at least a dozen Joes in the area, so most people just called him "The Indian." It worked. He liked it. I've no idea what he called some of us.

In the Forks area we had four John Johnsons, too. Rather than having to explain which one we were talking about, we named them by what they did or how they looked. The tall one we called Long John, the fat one was Fat John, the railroad man was Gandy John and the one who hauled coal to people's homes was Coal John. As I said, it worked.

Blackie had his snitches loafing about everywhere. Good-for-nothin' bums watching for something to report to him. He paid them in free drinks or a meal at Shannahan's, and ocassionally a dollar or two. If they hadn't seen me running in to Hymie's, it was still possible they might see me leaving.

"Hymie," I called to him. "Sell me a couple o' them big red bandanas ye got there. Maybe they'll think that's why I came in here, though I doubt it."

Outside, standing in front of the store, I took one of the big hankerchiefs out of the bag and gave my nose a good honk. I stuffed it into my pocket, walked to the tracks and turned west toward the gandy house, pretending to be checkin' the rails and ties as I went.

The gandy house was just a big shed. It housed workbenches, winches, hoists and such like, and my cubby-hole of an office. Rails led into it and it was big enough to drive an engine in for repairs. The section men – "gandy dancers" – stored the tools of their trade in the gandy house. Spikes, spike hammers, bolts, buckets, barrels of creosote and pitch, even a couple of hand pumper scooter cars. A roundhouse was being built to house all of this and would be ready by spring.

I was at the gandy house the next morning when one of Blackie's meal mooching snitches came to tell me that Blackie wanted to see me. The man stunk of whiskey and vomit, and he'd wet his britches sometime in the last day or so. A lovely class of people Blackie surrounded himself with.

I knew what Blackie wanted with me, but I knew better than to walk in to his office looking scared. So I came in smiling with my hand out as if expecting to be congratulated. There were three men in dark suits, ties and derbies – the uniform of an O'Rourke "gorilla."

The suits were no better quality than the men who wore them. Well-dressed bone breakers, they were. And it was my bones they were lookin' at just now.

Two of the "suits" were strangers to me, but the third was Slane Lattery, son of a dead dear friend, Jeremy, and a saintly mother, Elizabeth. Jeremy had been fireman on #7 on the Moorhead run when the boiler plugged and blew.

The explosion drove a steel plate into his chest and threw him backward into the tender car where he was scalded to death by steam from the boiler. A bad way to die. I told Elizabeth he died instantly. I don't think I'll go to hell for that one.

Now, an Irishman is an "opposite" sort of man. If the room is full of noisy people he enters quietly until he can get his bearings. On the other hand, if the room is quiet he puts out his hand and charges in leading with his mouth.

When I walked into Blackie's office his face was so grim it took away three days of sunlight, and the three black suits merely added to the darkness. You can bet I came through the door talking.

"Well, now, Blackie," I started. "Ye've no need to be thankin' me for meddlin' in your affairs, if that's what ye had in mind. It's a pleasure to be of service to ye." Blackie had all the warmth of a Dakota Territory blizzard across his face.

"Sit down, Will," he fairly snarled at me. I knew I would have to be a dancing master to get around him today. "Meddlin' is right," he growled. "Are ye thinkin' to cut yerself in on my business? Is that what you're up to? Or are ye just takin' care of a few old friends of yours? I'd like to hear what you're up to before I turn you over to my boys."

Pretending surprise I said, "Blackie! Are ye that far off that ye don't see the favor I've done for ye?" The blizzard remained on Blackie's face. He knew me too well to be surprised at my having a story ready for him. This was no time for a whiney defense so I charged full tilt into the face of that blizzard and the three dark suits.

"That big Swede," I was lookin' Blackie right in the eye. "Is the most popular and honest Norwegian Lutheran in the county. They all love him." Blackie started to speak but I cut him off. "If you had closed on his note it would have been all over the county by dark. Add to that the fact that you're Irish, an' Catholic t' boot, an' ye might as well fold yer tent. Ye'd be out o' business that quick."

Things that hit Blackie in the wallet registered hard and fast on him. He digested my "report" quickly, and swallowed whatever it was he'd been about to say. I jumped into the sudden silence with more of my own "logic."

Trying to make myself look aggressive and at the same time a little offended I said, "By the time I'd heard about your business with the Swede, you'd already sent your muscle boys off t' Ojata. There wasn't time to come lookin' fer ye. So I jist got the money and sent it on."

Blackie's brain was working so hard you could smell his hair burning. I had gotten the better of him before, just a little while ago, and he wasn't going to let it happen again if he could help it.

Before he could get set I played my ace. "One more thing I'd do if I was you. All them Lutherans are God fearin' and church goin'. Every Sunday they gather at the church just outside of Ojata. Spend most o' the day there, what with the services an' talkin' Norwegian an' picnickin' and steerin' their young people together." Blackie was listening but the blizzard was still there.

"If you was t' show up there," I suggested, "An' make a show of givin' the Swede back his money an' tellin' him – just loud enough for a few others t' hear – that he can take as long as he needs about payin' it back, that story'd be spread hell, west an' crooked by them stone-faced Norskes."

Blackie's blizzard was losing some of its force so I continued. "It'll do ye no end o' good, Blackie, an' besides, yer money's as safe as in your own pocket. The Swede wouldn't take it, anyway." And there I rested my case while more of Blackie's hair burned with deep thought.

It's always been difficult for me to sit still without looking as if I'd just stolen something, so I got to my feet and turned to look young Lattery in the eye. It was not a pleasant look I gave him. Black suit or no, he wilted like summer grass in a drought.

"I know yer Maa is proud of ye, but does she know what ye're doin' t' earn that suit ye're wearin'? And yer Daa. I'm that glad he's not here to see this." The boy cringed with guilt.

"Aw-right, Willum," Blackie's growl interupted my little sermon. Whenever he called me Willum I knew I was home safe. The jury was in and the verdict was not guilty. I had survived the blizzard. I tried to tell my knees they could quit shaking. Everything was all right. For now, anyway.

The Frog
Point Filly

I want to tell you about my friend Blackie and me and that little grey filly that was brought up from Frog Point just south of The Forks, but I have t' give you just a bit o' history first.

Blackie O'Rourke came to Grand Forks in the late 1870's. I call him my friend, and he is. Usually. My name is Willum Duffy, late of Ireland, now of Grand Forks by way o' St. Paul. I came in '80, but back in '76 the two of us were workin' on the St. Paul, Minneapolis & Manitoba Railroad out of the St. Paul yard when Blackie decided to leave the rails and try his luck in Dakota Territory.

Back then The Forks was just a few houses, a couple of saloons and a store or two, and two rivers – the Red and the Red Lake – comin' together. Blackie saw the opportunity and jumped right in. He opened a general merchandise store.

Now, about Blackie. He was half Irish, half heathen and 100% greedy. I said he was my friend and he is, but I know better than to play poker with him. During our early St. Paul days he saved my hide a time or two, and I saved his as well, which made us brothers . . . of a sort.

There were many times I was almighty glad to have him beside me, and other times when I paid dearly for the privilege. But if ever I was "under siege" I wanted him standin' back t' back with me. There wasn't much the two of us together couldn't handle. We worked and fought well together. But every time we shook hands I felt like countin' my fingers to see if I got 'em all back.

A few Irishers trickled into the Forks back then – Catholics, the lot of them – but they hardly slowed down on their way through looking for land to file on. But an Irisher is not a man t' be alone out on a windy, treeless plain with the nearest neighbor more than a mile beyond yellin' distance.

Many left their claims in a year or two and came back to town where they took up jobs as policemen, bartenders, politicians and various "public servants" of whatever kind. Anything, as long as it had people around.

Then came the Presbyterians, Methodists, Baptists and Episcopalians. Their nationalities didn't seem to matter to them as much as which church they went to. Got t' give them Protestants credit. They were good, honest men who knew how t' build.

In no time a'tall they had the Forks up and growin' smartly. Even so, they still counted their money twice after dealin' with each other. There's an old Irish quotation that goes, "Trust everybody, but cut the cards." Some o' those fellows woulda made good Irishmen. The U.S. government set up a post office and le Grand Fourche, as it had been called, officially became Grand Forks.

The rails got here in 1880 and brought m'self and the wives of these good merchants. The St.P.M.& M. crossed the Red River at Nashville (East Grand Forks they're callin' it now) and the Forks really began to change.

But that's not what I wanted to tell you about. All that history and such. It's about that litle filly from Frog Point that Blackie and I haggled over.

Frog Point was a pest hole of a place about twenty miles south of the Forks, along the river. A colorful collection of gamblers, thieves and 'companion ladies' and such. It was a port of call for the flat boats, deliverin' goods and passengers.

Blackie sent Nelly Breen – one of his dark-suited arm twistin' boys – down to Frog Point to collect on a bill that was owed him by one of the salooners. Nelly came back leadin' the tiniest, most beautiful little dapple grey filly y' could ever imagine. But no money..

Blackie hit the roof. He smoked up the air with more profanity than the Baptists and Lutherans knew existed. The Methodists and Presbyterians were impressed. The 'Piscopalians grinned and pretended to be shocked. Most of the Irish didn't even blink.

Blackie wanted the money! Evidently the bill was a fair size. He threatened to sic the rest of his dark suits on poor Nelly, who thought he'd made a pretty good deal gettin' even the little horse out of the salooner, seein' as how the fortunes of the town had sort of slipped when Big Jim Hill moved his Great Northern railroad off the river banks and over to the town of Hillsboro. But there I go with more history.

There were good citizens in Frog Point, too. Folks who got their groceries and mail there. Mostly farmers who lived a ways out of town. But whenever the little town got talked about, the good citizens were never mentioned. It was always the "scarlet" element that held center stage.

The story goes that the postmaster thought he'd do his civic bit to improve the local reputation so he changed the town's name to Bellmont. People kept spellin' it with only one 'l' and pretty soon the postmaster gave up. So the road goin' south out o' the Forks got named Belmont Road instead of Frog Point Alley or some such thing. Ah, damn me. More history.

Anyway, Nelly came runnin' into my roundhouse this p'ticular day lookin' for help. Or a hole to climb into or a boxcar headin' out o' town. He had the filly with him, and I fell in love with that little darlin' the minute I laid eyes on her, she was that fine.

A dainty little dancer and beautifully made, she looked more like a toy than a real horse. The muscles of her narrow chest were smooth and hard, and she had a lovely, well-rounded little rump that put me in mind of of a lass I knew back in St. Paul. Tailor-made for pullin' a small shay, she was. It's the filly I'm talkin' about, now.

My lovin' wife Liddy had just brought me lunch when Nelly came in. She saw the little grey and, just like me, she fell in love on the spot.

"Oh, Will," she cooed at me in that little way o' hers that tells me I'm about t' say yes to something. "Isn't she beautiful. What a lovely cart pony she'd make for us." You can pretty well guess what I was going t' have do about that.

Back in our St. Paul days Liddy's dad tried to pair her off with Blackie thinkin' he'd be the better provider. But my sweet Liddy made the wiser choice. She walked down the aisle with me, and Blackie went down the road unrequited.

Secretly, I think he was relieved not to be anchored to any woman, but he made a point of tellin' me, too often and too loud, how he had been crushed by Liddy's rebuff. Malarkey!

Nelly stayed safely at the roundhouse while I led the little grey back to Blackie's shop on Third Street just north o' the tracks where Blackie sold his groceries, patent medicines and an odd assortment of things. The sign over his door read MERCANTILE, but he bragged that he dealt in hardware, harness, hand guns and hooch.

He also advertised himself as an undertaker. Nobody else wanted that job so nobody asked to see his credentials. If you brought an expired relative to Blackie, you got him back in a day or so in a pine box with the lid nailed down tight. You were never quite sure if you were burying a body or a carcass.

Anyway, I tied the dapple to the post out front, went inside and straight on back to his office. I don't know what Blackie had against lettin' sunlight into that area but the place had all the cheer of a Lutheran funeral. The windows were not just wearing curtains. They had quilts! No peeping Toms around here. Dark as a tomb, it was.

My mouth was already in gear when I walked through his door. "Blackie," I sang out. "What are ye askin' fer that skinny little thing Nelly brought back from Frog Point? My wife is showin' an interest. And by the way, just what sort of animal is it, anyway?" I already knew. I was just makin' conversation.

He had his head down pretending to be writin' somethin' important in one of his ledgers, like he didn't want t' talk to me. But his head snapped up at my question. "Why y' bloody fool. It's a horse! Can't y' see that? It's a horse! And a mighty small one, at that."

As I've said time and again, when it comes t' bein' Irish, Blackie can be an embarrassment at times. Any Irishman worth his salt could have told you that the little animal was a cross between a Welsh pony and an Arabian. T'was the Welsh blood line made her all that small, but it was the Arabian head and body lines that made her beautiful.

But Blackie wasn't bein' Irish just then. He was too busy bein' greedy. About the money Nelly Breen did not bring back from Frog Point – or Bellmont. – or Belmont. Whatever.

Whenever Blackie wanted me for something he liked to send one of his "dark suits" after me t' make me hurry right over. That way he could keep me off balance, so t' speak. But when I showed up unexpected he didn't like it a'tall 'cause he knew I already had my case prepared, leavin' him t' be the one standin' on a stool with one short leg, so t' speak.

The best way t' get Blackie's mind off any subject was to put money on the table. "I could give ye maybe fifty dollars for her," I offered.

"Fifty," he snorted! "She's worth a hundred, if a dime." Just a minute ago the little pony was worthless to him, but now money had entered the picture.

I made a show of pause and deliberation before conceding, "I could maybe go sixty, if y'd throw in that little two-wheeled rig y' took in on a trade last summer. It's doin' you little good sittin' in your back lot."

"Sixty? Never! And that's an end to it." He turned his back to me.

Blackie was a marvelous actor. Such a one for dramatics, he was. The only thing he liked more than gettin' the better of me was the hagglin' we did. And it hardly mattered what we haggled over. I knew he wasn't going t' let me walk out the door without onc more attempt.

"Ah, y're prob'ly right, Blackie," I pretended to concede. "Anyway, y'll likely find another taker soon enough. You're right about her size, though. She's pretty but she is small. I left her tied to the post out front. . . in the sun. She'll most prob'ly need feedin' and waterin' before y' put her inside your fence."

Blackie's pasture was west of town a mile or so. I didn't think he'd have time just now for taking the little filly out there. I made it to the door before he took the bait.

"Seventy-five," sez Blackie. "And you can have the damn two-wheeler. But I'll take it in cash money, thank ye! And y' can tell your lovely wife that it's only 'cause I still love her that I'm bein' that good to ye." It was a bloody lie, but he knew it rankled me to hear him say it.

I paused in the doorway hoping the back o' my head looked as if I was considering the deal. The truth of it was I had to get my face under control. I couldn't turn around and let him see my grin. "I'll take her," sez I.

About The Author

G.L. (Jerry) O'Connor is an educator (over 30 years in the junior high classroom), a humorous speaker (over 30 years on the banquet circuit), a raconteur (life-long story teller of tall tales, soft lies and good jokes) and an entrepreneur (makes and markets the world's greatest Mustard).

He is an over-the-hill North Dakota native descended from territorial pioneers. He grew up in a loud and wonderful family of twelve children where he learned to shout, defend himself and, now and then, ask permission. Jerry and his wife of forty-plus years have raised three of their own.

He earned his Bachelor's degree from the University of North Dakota (he's a Fighting Sioux) and his Master's Degree from Texas A&M (Yep, he's an Aggie, too.). If you add up all the years, he has spent over half his life in the classroom.

Now that he's retired, Jerry has more time to spend writing. He has completed his first full-length novel (a western), a shorter novelette (also a western) and a novelette for young readers (a mystical fantasy adventure). He has also written articles and poems, most of which have not been published...yet.